TABLE OF CONTENTS

Ghost Stories of the Lehigh Valley

•

Charles J. Adams III
David J. Seibold

Exeter House Books
1993

GHOST STORIES
of the LEHIGH VALLEY

EXETER HOUSE BOOKS
P.O. Box 6411
Wyomissing, Pennsylvania 19610

PRINTED IN THE UNITED STATES OF AMERICA

ISBN: 978-1-880683-02-6

Lehigh Valley Ghost Stories

INTRODUCTION

You have heard the tales. As a child, they were told around crackling campfires or by family elders.

They are the stories which linger with you for the rest of your life.

They are the *ghost* stories.

Who has not told and re-told ghost stories? Some of the greatest literature of our time and before it has at its core the notion that there is an everlasting life somewhere in a great beyond. In another dimension, ghosts return to earth to accomplish what their mortal beings could not.

They haunt.

They go bump in the night.

They strike fear in all our hearts and souls.

They are *ghosts.*

You would not have purchased this book if you did not have some basic interest in the notion that ghosts may well inhabit our space and time.

Beyond this, however, this volume will bring to light another, perhaps even more disconcerting, possibility--that the Lehigh Valley is literally alive (so to speak) with ghosts.

Lehigh Valley Ghost Stories

If nothing else, Lehigh, Northampton and Carbon Counties do abound with ghost *stories*. As you read these tales, remember that they are told by your neighbors, and maybe your own relatives and friends.

These are the ghost stories from your own backyard. These are Lehigh Valley Ghost Stories. We hope you enjoy them.

Our quest for ghostly events and encounters dates into the 1970s. After hundreds of investigations and interviews, it has become obvious that, barring mass and calculated fabrication and/or hysteria, something does indeed exist in that usually invisible, inaudible and undetectable dimension.

Our investigations bore literary fruit in 1982 with the publication of "Ghost Stories of Berks County." So rich was this single county with ghostly lore that two more volumes on Berks ghosts followed.

After researching and publishing books on shipwrecks and sea stories along the New Jersey and Delaware coasts, we ventured back into the spirit realm with the release of ghost books in Delaware, Cape May and the Poconos.

At first glance, the notion of ghosts wandering the Lehigh Valley may fly in the face of many impressions of the region.

A dynamic metropolitan area which stretches along busy transportation corridors, the Lehigh Valley as a commercial and statistical area is the mini-megalopolis of the cities of Allentown, Bethlehem and

Lehigh Valley Ghost Stories

Easton.

In recent decades, this region has experienced growth and progress. It has risen above many challenges and has made the painful transition from being a center of heavy manufacturing to a more service and technology-based economy.

The visitors view of the valley is that of busy highways, crowded shopping malls and prosperous urban centers.

But in the midst of this activity, ghosts glide silently among the living.

They inhabit not only deep glens and darkened country settings, they inhabit office buildings in cities, university buildings, restaurants and very public facilities.

The questions we, as "ghost hunters" are asked most often are (a) Do ghostly encounters follow any particular pattern? and (b) Do you believe that ghosts really do exist?

In order to set the stage for the stories which follow, let us then lay the foundation with brief answers to those questions.

Are there any similarities or patterns in the reports of supernatural occurrences?

Yes and no.

No, in that ghosts, poltergeists, or whatever one chooses to call them show up in all cultures and times.

Be it a Jamaican duppy or an Irish banshee, a ghost is a key player in popular and classic literature in

3

virtually every country and society of the world.

Thus, the pattern forms a blanket across time and distance.

More specifically, however, there are similarities in many of the stories we have researched in the mid-Atlantic states.

Those who have told their tales have spanned all age, class, color and ethnic groups. The stories have also come from city, suburb and countryside; in old home and new, commercial properties, and even mobile homes.

There seems, then, to be no rhyme or reason to the placement of the ghosts--no one thread which may run through the geographic or demographic considerations.

It was only after the first few dozen exhaustive interviews that a pattern actually *was* discovered.

As it turned out, that pattern was surprisingly simple, and possibly very much part and parcel to an answer to the second most-asked question of a ghost story researcher.

In virtually every home, shop, office, theater or barn visited, one fact emerged. After a while, that fact was paired with a reasonable theory on the very existence of ghosts, and an interesting correlation could be made.

That one salient fact was that in these places, some sort of renovations, additions, modifications or remodeling had been done.

Those projects, in those places, may well have been the kindling for the phantasmagoric flames which followed.

What could then lead to an "explanation" of ghostly happenings is fascinating to ponder.

Science has taught us that matter cannot be destroyed.

Medicine has taught us that our bodies are more than flesh, blood and bone. Within our beings are charges of electricity which spark our nervous reactions.

When a human being breathes no more, when the heart stops and the brain ceases to function, the flesh, blood and bone is left to decompose.

But what of those electrical charges? If they cannot be destroyed, then what becomes of them?

There are those far more intelligent than we who claim to have proof that these charges--these minuscule flashes of energy--escape the body at the time of severe trauma (death, of course, being the most severe), and remain earthbound not so much in ghostly form but in scientifically verifiable form.

Think of a tape recorder, audio or video. Think of the complicated, technological and yet quite simple way sound vibrations or light projections are transferred to and recorded on audio or video tape.

Recording tape is basically a form of rust on a form of plastic. The audible and visual images are imprinted on that rust, on that tape, and retained.

That tape can be held up to light, scratched, exposed to water, whatever--and it will not release its images.

It takes a flick of the finger on the "playback" button to reveal what was recorded, essentially on rust.

Could it not be that essentially this same process is what "records" ghosts?

Depending on your outlook, the premise is either ridiculously simple or outlandish.

But, let's say that weak but very real electrical energy is released from a body at a traumatic time. Shards of thoughts, concepts and subconscious information burst from the brain and escape into the atmosphere.

Let's say this energy finds a host upon which to "record" itself. Following the recording tape theory, let's say that host is rust. A rusty nail, perhaps.

During renovations, it is likely that old nails or old, rusty appurtenances are exposed. Also exposed are the "recordings" made on them.

The only missing link in the process is the "playback" mechanism.

This is where the "psychic" or "medium" comes in.

The familiar perception of a psychic is that of a slightly off-center, "cloak and candle" type who dwells within a mysterious, dark world.

In reality, a psychic could be anyone--your best

friend, your cousin, your next-door neighbor, your boss, and yes, even you!

We all possess some level of psychic power. Some of us can vividly recall dreams. Some can predict or sense events before they occur through premonitions. Some experience "deja vu," or the feeling that what happens in one instance has happened before.

Some of us can detect the presence of a ghost.

These people, who are blessed (or cursed) with the highest psychic powers, are the "playback buttons" on the tape recorder of the supernatural.

Through their unique sense, they can read those bits of information left over from a previous life. They can piece together parts of a puzzle which cannot be seen, heard or felt by the majority of those around them.

There is no formal schooling which enables one to acquire this sense. It can be heightened or fine-tuned, but as with the ability to be a virtuoso on the cello or a home run hitter, much of it is in-born and, if you will, a "gift."

Interestingly, most people never know they are "psychic" until a profound event takes place which alerts them to the fact.

They may hear an unexplainable noise, see a shadowy form or sense an icy chill. They try to alert others, but their observations fall on deaf ears and doubting minds. Most people are uncomfortable with, and thus tend to deny the existence of something beyond their comprehension or outside the limitations of their senses of sight, sound, touch, and thought.

People caught unaware of their psychic powers become those who are regarded as a bit off-center, or just, plain crazy. Those who are incapable of reaching beyond or even understanding the supernatural hold whose who are in suspicion and, too often, contempt.

Do ghosts exist? Religion tends to purport, and science tends to support the proposition that they do.

The ghosts among us are not wandering souls with unfinished business here on earth. They do not torment and threaten with rattling chains and outstretched, bony fingers.

One need not wait under a full moon or on the anniversary of a tragedy to witness these spirits. They are all around us.

Science and technology can be applied in another way to all of this.

As you read this right now, there are faces and voices all around you. They dash in front of your eyes, between your face and the book. They weave around your shoulders and thrust into and through your mortal body.

These phantom faces and voices will be beside you in bed tonight. They will sit next to you at the breakfast table, and ride in the back seat of your car tomorrow.

Don't turn around, *they're here*, and you cannot

escape them.

You have in your possession an electronic device which can detect and actually identify these invisible faces and voices which whirl around you right now.

Turn on your radio, or your television. They will emerge from the atmosphere. They are not ghosts, they are images pulled from the air around you. Stand between the transmitter and the receiver, and the faces and voices penetrate you. Try to capture them in any other way but on tape, on rust, and they will elude you.

If, then, these faces and voices which are far beyond your grasp except through extraordinary means, can be identified, is it not possible--at least possible--that there do exist, in another dimension, even more faces and voices?

Do ghosts exist?

Only you can, and someday will, answer that question.

Sleep tight tonight!

Charles J. Adams III
Reading, Pa., May 1, 1993

THE LADY IN WHITE

𝕋alk to folks around Walnutport about ghosts, and it's likely somebody will come up with the tale of the "Lady in White."

That's what they call the mysterious wraith who is said to walk along the towpath of the old Lehigh Canal.

Some strange powers and bizarre episodes have been attached to this pallid wraith since stories of her, or its, existence started to surface.

The Lady in White has been discussed quietly in Walnutport since at least the 1940s, and in more recent years, her exploits have taken some interesting turns.

Everet Kaul, a trustee of the Lehigh Canal Association, recalled stories told to him by the late Frank Kelchner, who was a boatman on the waterway which was once a lifeline of transportation in the Lehigh Valley.

Kelchner would speak of a strange woman, clad all in white and perhaps an albino herself, who would walk along the towpath of the canal.

That towpath was normally the domain of mules

who tugged the boats up and down the canal. Kelchner, who was also once the locktender at the Walnutport lock house, claimed the mules actually passed right through the ghostly form when they crossed paths.

Even the chief of police in nearby Slatington recalled the tales of the Lady in White.

Chief Ted Kistler thought back to his high school years as he retraced the story as told to him.

"I graduated in '61," he said. "There was supposed to be some woman dressed in white and walking on the water."

The chief also recalled a large, abandoned house along the canal in Walnutport, a house the locals claimed was haunted. It was located near where the Lady in White was often reported, near what was Lock No. 23 of the canal.

The story reached into another generation as Tammy Piparato discussed the ghost story while she toiled at the Anchor Inn in Walnutport.

"A gentleman would tell me that when he was younger, and supposedly even now, there was this 'White Lady,' or 'Lady in White' who walks across the canal here," she said.

"She just walks right out and she floats right above the water. The kids used to see her, and the older people who used to live down here used to see her, too. I have never seen her personally, but that's what they tell me."

Margie Waylan has also heard the stories. "I

remember that a woman was seen all in white, walking on the canal. Everybody was sort of scared, you know, because there was this *ghost,* all in white, walking there. I remember, it was about 25 years ago. I was in my late teens or early twenties when this happened.

"People would walk up and down, along the canal, looking for her," she continued.

Margie said the local police were well aware of the story, and those who ventured to the canal to see what they could see. "Oh, they were upset. For a small town, it was a big thing. There was even a story about a guy who fell into the canal water because the ghost chased him.

"Oh, everybody came from miles around," Margie continued. They had to hire extra police because everybody wanted to see the canal at night. The police would go crazy. They'd say, 'go back, go back, there's nothing.'

"There were hundreds of people here. You couldn't even park. They were all looking for the Lady in White!"

The story of the Lady in White may have stemmed from a seed of fact. That fact has long since been obscured by exploitation, exaggeration and even playful hoaxes.

Those around Walnutport treat the basic premise of this transparent image of a woman on the canal bank as perhaps more than just a legend. And yet, they know that the fertile imaginations of those seeking to torpedo the tale have stretched the story to the limits of credibility.

Mickey Roper chuckled as he recalled the time in the 1940s when he was working at the Kearns Lumber Company.

He said he "borrowed" a mannequin from a store in Northampton, carted it back in the lumber company truck, and propped it up on the bank of the Lehigh River.

The river rose, the mannequin broke from its dirt mooring and floated freely downstream until it became caught in a dam.

This, Mickey said, caused quite a commotion because folks along the shore believed the floating form to be everything from a dead body to the Lady in White!

Was there, is there, a Lady in White who walks the area of the old canal in Walnutport? Nobody knows for certain.

But should you venture to the area of old Lock No. 23 some dark night, beware of who may be following you!

•

CHELSEA, THE GHOST OF CATASAUQUA

"**W**e're near a cemetery."

That's all Jenny will allow us to divulge regarding the exact location of the pleasant home in Catasauqua where a ghost named Chelsea has teased, tormented and nearly terrified a young family for several years.

Before their story, a brief explanation about an uncomfortable, but very real fact of a ghost story writer's life.

While the following incident does take place in Catasauqua, the street address will not be published. And, while we refer to the protagonist in the story as "Jenny," it is not her real name.

It is an example of a story given in exchange for anonymity.

For the writer and reader, it is a trade-off of sorts. The story would go unpublished because of the very understandable reluctance of the subjects to release their true names and correct addresses.

They fear more the wrath of a curious public

than the ghostly events they live with every day.

They also fear the possible loss of property value, the acts of unthinking vandals and ridicule by those with whom they associate on a daily basis. Thus, in the process of gathering ghost stories, the authors respect the privacy of their sources and comply with their wishes.

Jenny isn't certain if her home's proximity to the cemetery has anything to do with the presence which has made its way into their lives.

She recalled one of the first incidents. It was in 1990.

"We were both sleeping, and at the same time we both looked up," she said. "Twelve o'clock at night, and we both looked up!

"We didn't say anything to each other until the whole experience was over, but we each heard somebody coming up the steps and then we looked, and there was a figure. I didn't see a face, or eyes, or anything like that. It was just all black.

"I was looking over by the bannister. We both looked up at each other. My husband grabbed a mug and we went down the steps. We never heard anything go back down the steps.

"We went downstairs to check all the doors and windows. They were all locked, so it couldn't have been an intruder. Then, we were back upstairs. We both saw the same thing. We both couldn't possibly be having the same dream!"

Jenny said she wasn't actually afraid at the time of that first encounter, but further incidents gave her cause for concern.

One time, a toy telephone began ringing. That would be nothing unusual would it not have been for the fact that there were no batteries in the toy at the time.

"My husband would place things on the wall, and they would move," she remembered. As firmly as he would secure them to the wall, they would still move as if some unearthly force was setting them in motion.

"He thinks it's a girl, and her name is Chelsea," Jenny said of her husband's acceptance of the spirit. "It, or she, would pick on him at nighttime."

Such a situation might be awkward for a wife to accept, even if the flirting female is of the phantom variety.

"Oh, no," said Jenny. "I think she watches over me. She picks on him, though, because she knows I don't feel threatened."

On one occasion, Jenny believes she actually saw Chelsea's form pass by her. "It was a silhouette. I didn't see a face. It could have almost been a big sweatsuit jacket, but all enclosed." She struggled to describe the ghostly figure.

"Nobody believes any of this," she affirmed, but indicated that it didn't really matter to Jenny and her husband what others thought.

"We really don't tell anybody any more," she said. "We're near a cemetery, nobody has ever died in our home, maybe it's a relative of mine or something. I really don't know."

As it turns out, her husband admitted to have felt the presence of the spirit long before they shared that frightening experience in the middle of the night in 1990.

Jenny and her mate believe they have shielded their two children from the spectral activity in their home.

"I know that if they knew," Jenny said, "they wouldn't be able to sleep."

She's probably right.

•

In Pennsylvania German folklore, and in the dialect, the following exhortations are given to protect those who encounter a ghost:
"Ihr Hellengeischder geht ihr heraus!
Des is Gotteshaus!"
Or, in English,
"Spirit of Hell be gone! This is God's house!"

HEXENKOPF:
MISERY MOUNTAIN

With its rich Pennsylvania "Dutch" heritage and foreboding landscape, many sections of the Lehigh Valley cling to the ancient traditions of "hexerei," "powwowing" and, in laymen's terms, "witchcraft."

Those traditions are deeply rooted in history and culture, and while many of the beliefs and practices have faded, their legacies and legends linger in dusty books and manuscripts and the fertile minds of the elder residents of the region.

Over the more than two centuries of its existence, these captivating tales of curses, cures and communions with "the other side" have found their way into barroom banter and scholarly chronicles.

Many of the most substantial stories of this darker side of the Pennsylvania Dutch were recorded in the dialect--a lyrical corruption of German and English which is still spoken by a small number of Lehigh Valley residents.

Indeed, the origins of some of the deepest of the occult practices can be traced to ancient Germany, where such events as Walpurgis Nacht brought the fear of the power of the underworld to the villages and countryside of the Rhine River valley.

On this evening, April 30, folks would prepare bonfires and other distractions which would ward off the evil spirits and witches who were said to roam at midnight.

The custom was brought to the New World by German immigrants, and was continued as they settled into their new homes.

Just west of Virginville, Berks County, is a ridge (along, of all things, "Witchcraft Road") which the locals refer to as "Hexe Danz," or the Witches' Dance.

Also called "Witches' Hill," the otherwise unremarkable mound is where eerie, bobbing lights have been seen, where crops won't grow, and where a mysterious power once spooked horses and now causes a car's engine to stop for no apparent reason.

The Lehigh Valley has its own Witches' Dance, but it is a cluster of rocks in Williams Township, near Raubsville.

They call it Hexenkopf, and even in the enlightened twentieth century, there are those who will blame their misfortunes on the antics of the witches who dwell in the rocks of the hill whose name translates to Witches' Head.

Poking more than 800 feet over Stout's Valley, the hill's mysteries can also be traced to the old

German beliefs in necromancy.

In his writings, Northampton County historian Matthew Henry told of witches who were seen with their arms locked together, dancing in a circles around a sturdy oak tree at the summit of Hexenkopf.

He wrote of unearthly sounds which emanated from the hill, and of ghostly lights which glowed on the ridge.

Charles E. Boyd, in his research on the history of Williams Township, claimed the reputed "powers" of Hexenkopf were first tapped by Dr. Peter Saylor, who practiced powwowing in the Raubsville area in the early part of the 19th century.

"While many exorcists used objects like a chair, an animal or, if handy, a corpse as receptors for the evils which they drew out from the patient under treatment, Dr. Saylor conceived the notion of using Hexenkopf as his gigantic receptor," Boyd reported.

It is said that Saylor tapped into the very bowels of the mountain for his power as he did much of his work in or near a cave near his home on the side of Hexenkopf.

A second-generation powwower, Saylor also apparently capitalized on the natural character of the hill when he cast his spell over those who came to partake of his talents.

Scattered deposits of mica on the rocks of Hexenkopf made it glitter in the moonlight. As Boyd said, "local people looked upon Hexenkopf as they would have looked upon the throne of the the Evil One Himself!"

Saylor passed on his "gift" to John H. Wilhelm, a neighbor, and the Wilhelm family continued the powwowing tradition of the Saylors. Local lore tells of crowds of buggies and people in tiny Raubsville as those hoping to partake of powwow healing assembled there.

One newspaper article claimed, "Many times at early dawn of the first Friday in the new moon, Raubsville was crowded with teams and vehicles of every description.

Powwowing gradually faded away in Raubsville, and the last known faith-healer who practiced in the grand Pennsylvania German tradition died in about 1950.

The powwowers and their patients in Williams Township were the central characters in a minor novel, "The Hex Woman," written by Earl Joseph ("Raube") Walters in 1931.

Much more serious documentation on whatever mysteries Hexenkopf holds is the evidence which indicates that a woman may actually have been taken to court after being charged with practicing witchcraft.

In a paper, "Hexenkopf: Mystery, Myth and Legend," Prof. Ned Heindel cited an 1863 article in a religious publication, in which Rev. Charles P. Krauth recounted the legends of Hexenkopf, and further claimed that the witches "did not always escape with impunity."

Rev. Krauth quoted an court document in which jurors were given the case of a Williams Township, Northampton County widow who "did commit certain most wicked acts (called enchantments and charms)...maliciously and diabolically against a certain white horse."

The court paper, published with the names of the plaintiff and defendant and the exact dates omitted, noted that the accused, S_____ B_____, "at first resolutely denied the charge; but the learned judges at last convinced her of her guilt, and she always confessed herself a witch, though she was unable to say in what manner her enchantments had been performed."

The woman was punished with one year imprisonment and "every quarter to stand six hours in the pillory."

Dr. Heindel attempted to track down the court records at the Northampton County courthouse, but faced a disorganized, unindexed batch of 18th and 19th century transcripts and failed to locate the original paper.

Other stories of "hexerei" and the supernatural have circulated around Williams Township for generations.

A bedraggled old woman once wandered around the countryside, asking for sustenance at every farmhouse she reached. Believing she was a witch, the farmers obliged.

An old man had a vision of the ghost of his daughter, who told him to hasten to Hexenkopf, where he would find a fortune buried at a certain spot.

He followed the spirit's instructions, and after digging furiously at the prescribed location, he was frightened out of his boots by the booming voice of a massive figure in white which warned him to leave or face horrible consequences.

One story which involves Hexenkopf tells of the ghost of a peg-legged man which can be seen just after dusk on the hill. It is the spirit of a farmer who tumbled from the rocks to his death while pursuing a witch. This wraith, nicknamed "Farmer Brown," is said to have tousled, gray hair and a long beard. His ghost is easily recognizable by the eerie tapping of his wooden leg on the rocks.

An old folk tale around what some have called "Misery Mountain" also speaks of the ghosts of two farmers who, in life, engaged in a volatile dispute over a property line on Hexenkopf.

After both men passed on, their feud continued, taking the shape of terrible bolts of fire and a putrid stench which can be discerned from time to time on the hill.

A headless hunter and his companion, an equally decapitated dog, have been seen wandering on Hexenkopf, and an unearthly, elusive white fox has befuddled marksmen on the hill for decades.

Lehigh Valley Ghost Stories

While the stories of the hauntings of Hexenkopf have been diluted, and sometimes discredited by time, there are those who live around "Misery Mountain" who will never discount its powers.

"I won't venture to the rocks at night, and positively not on Halloween," says Jane Knapp.

The woman lives on Hexenkopf Road, and her reason for avoiding any confrontations with the powers that may or may not be on the mountain stem from some very personal experiences.

"On Halloween, many years ago," she said, "Robert Seip, of New Jersey, asked his sister, Dorothy Knapp, if he could host a party at her home.

"Her house was more accommodating for a large group, and was located across the street from Hexenkopf Rock. During the course of the party, at midnight, Bob and a few of his friends wanted to walk over to the rock to add to the mystique of Halloween.

"The Halloween party took place, and at midnight, as planned, a few people went up to the rock. Not one of the local Williams Township natives even considered venturing to the rocks for fear of the witches."

Knapp was firm in her conviction regarding that mountain, and its witches. "It was like a superstition, but, it used to be that Witch Doctors would take evil spirits up to the rock and dump them off there, supposedly. If you irritate them, or make them angry, they get back at you."

24

She has reason to believe that claim.

Following their little jaunt to the haunted rock, all returned, and continued with their Halloween festivities.

"Several weeks later," Knapp continued, "many mishaps and tragedies followed. There was a thunder and lightning storm, and it knocked a tree down that missed a neighbor's home by a couple feet. That same neighbor, who lived in back of the house where the party was held, was working at a department store and one day when she was loading things on a shelf, things fell down and hit her, and she had to go to the hospital."

Another of the adventurers later suffered a hernia and needed treatment. Still another suffered the loss of his pet dog, which was struck by a car about a week after his master's Halloween hike on Hexenkopf.

Jane Knapp's personal recollections of the hill are enhanced by the lurid stories which have swirled around Williams Township for decades.

"There was a blind girl who climbed the rock," she recalled. "She had fallen down, and where she had fallen, you can see the outline of a witch's head on the rocks. A lot of people can see it, a certain way you look at it. It looks like the shape of the head of a witch."

She admitted that many people are still frightened of Hexenkopf, especially at night.

"Oh, yeah," she said, "they're superstitious.

They respect the witches.

"One may say this is just a story," Jane affirmed, "but I will not venture to the rocks at night, and positively not on Halloween. I just hope the witches don't get upset for telling the story."

•

At the old Black Horse Saloon, on Route 611, south of Easton, they called their ghost "Johnny the Wop."

The noisy, pesky spirit which was felt in the building when it was a popular tavern, is said to be that of a Prohibition-era mobster who was gunned down there.

The story includes a legend that the ghost remains there to guard a large sum of money which was hidden away just before "Johnny" was killed.

The building has a second ghost, as well. Locals say the spirit of a young boy has been seen walking aimlessly inside the old tavern.

...local legend

THE GLOWING TOMBSTONE

IN MEMORY OF SAMUEL GRABER
DIED OCTOBER 28, 1885
AGE 8 YEARS, 10 MONTHS, 20 DAYS

MARY ANN SHADE GRABER
DIED SEPTEMBER 5, 1885
AGE 3 YEARS, 8 MONTHS, 27 DAYS

MARTHA AVA GRABER
DIED JANUARY 29, 1896
AGE 9 YEARS, 1 MONTH, 6 DAYS

The texts of the tombstones tell the story. Three children, same family, all died within months, cut down in the prime of their youth by diphtheria.

The children rest for an eternity next to their parents, whose names are also inscribed on the handsome monument in the picturesque cemetery:

JAMES E. GRABER, M.D.
DIED OCTOBER 6, 1919
AGE 74 YEARS, 3 MONTHS, 24 DAYS

EMMA E. GRABER
DIED JUNE 18, 1937
AGE 84 YEARS, 8 MONTHS, 1 DAY

Lehigh Valley Ghost Stories

Five graves spread out around the stately monument. And, it is said that when the moonlight is right, preferably under a full moon, an eerie glow is cast upon the monument.

The phenomenon, and whatever it may mean, has captured the imaginations of many people around the little village of Steinsville, in the northwestern corner of Lehigh County.

"We have both seen the lights," said Charlotte McFarland.

Charlotte and Harold McFarland are Christian missionaries who have owned the former hotel in town since 1988.

They also own the property which surrounds the Graber family cemetery.

The McFarlands came to the country from their native Philadelphia and purchased the old Steinsville Hotel.

Built in 1832 by John and Catherine Stein, the building was once a stagecoach stop, and was frequented by men working in nearby slate quarries. It was later occupied by W.P.A. employees and then owned by the county.

The McFarlands converted the old hotel into their home, and they hope to convert a small stone building at the cemetery into a private meditation or worship refuge.

Local lore has it that when the state of Pennsylvania was searching for a site for a new

Normal School (college), Steinsville was considered as a location. Eventually, Kutztown was selected, and Steinsville never became a "college town."

Today, the crossroads cluster of houses and the hotel is bypassed by Route 143 and is barely noticeable to the casual traveler.

But should anyone stop by the old Graber burial plot under the right conditions, the spirit (or spirits) of the cemetery may make their presences known.

"It is spectacular," said Charlotte McFarland. "In the daytime, in regular light, you can't see anything in there which would indicate light."

However, both she and her husband said they have witnessed the strange glow in the cemetery at just about sunset.

They are not the only folks in the area who have seen the phenomenon.

Paul and Ruth Nester recalled the old stories about Dr. Graber and his family. The children succumbed to diphtheria in an age before immunizations, and Paul Nester discussed a sixth body buried in the graveyard.

"In 1938 or '39," he said, "they shipped somebody in there. It was somebody who was not a part of the family."

The grave is that of James F. Long, who died in 1909, according to the tombstone. Still, Paul Nester recalled witnessing a burial there.

"The guy who dug that grave was a big,

strapping stone mason who smoked three to four packs of cigarettes a day--and he lived to be 84 years old!

"My father was an undertaker in his time. They didn't do any embalming. They had ice caskets. They'd ice 'em up until shortly before the funeral. Then, they were all dressed up. If they smelled a little bit, that was OK."

Paul's recollections became germane to the story when he pointed out that the small building the McFarlands hope to use for meditation was once an ice house, where the ice used to pack the bodies was once stored, and where bodies were kept in winter when it was impossible to dig graves in the frozen ground.

Ruth Nester has seen the bizarre glow which is cast upon the monument in the Graber cemetery.

"It's beautiful," she remarked. "As the moon comes around, it shines on that big monument. You see five candles. It's really something to see it."

Mrs. Nester said several of her friends have seen the glow, which takes the shape of five candles.

Some say it is merely a coincidental reflection of the moonlight cast off the tombstones.

But, some say the five candle-shaped images represent the five Graber family members who are interred in the graveyard, perhaps an eerie manifestation of the three children who crossed to the other side far too soon, and of the man and woman who loved them so.

Lehigh Valley Ghost Stories

You see, local legend has it that after the good doctor's children perished, the folks in the area shunned him. How could he save them, they believed, if he was powerless to save his own offspring?

A dejected Dr. Graber vowed that someday they would understand, he would be vindicated, and even if in death, his Lord would give the naysayers a sign.

•

A recurring name in Lehigh Valley folklore is that of "Eileschpijjel," who is a somewhat rascally character who teases and challenges the Devil, plays pranks on the mortals, and pops up often in stories once told around campfires and now relegated to dusty, old books and the memories of the area's older residents.

Also spelled "Eilenshpiggel," "Eideschpiggel" and "Eire Schpickel," the mythical gent is said to have been based on Till Eulenspiegel, a 13th century German comic character.

Until the mid-20th century, Eileschpijjel stories were widely circulated throughout the Lehigh Valley and beyond.

THE OLD MAN'S IMAGE

The eye can play tricks with the imagination, as perhaps witnessed in the previous story.

In a popular Palmerton-area bar on Mauch Chunk Road, known to the locals as "Hazard Road," a peculiar configuration of wrinkles is said to be the eternal imprint of the spirit of a man who once owned what is now the Rusty Nail bar.

"You look at it, you can see a man's face in that leather," said Kenny Henritzy, who says he, his wife, and anyone who takes even a casual look at the cabinet door in question.

"It's from the man who originally owned the place, from what I understand. From the crinkles in the leather, you can actually see a man's face."

The leather upholstery covers a cabinet door near the cash register in the center of the barroom.

"The man who used to own that bar committed suicide in the place. After he was gone, this piece of leather stretched, wrinkled or pulled. You can actually see the face of the man who owned this place in that leather."

Lehigh Valley Ghost Stories

The upholstery has been touched up, cleaned and redone over the years, but still the face of the old man returns within its wrinkles.

Millie Slanina, who with her husband, Joseph, owns the Rusty Nail, confirmed the local legend.

"All I know is that it was supposed to have appeared after the prior owner owned it. And, it was supposed to have appeared on the door."

Millie said the former owner who supposedly left his imprint in the bar killed himself somewhere on the premises.

"And, it appeared here after he died," she added, referring to the leathery image.

"There's one lady who won't even come in here because of that face on the door," Millie concluded.

•

BUCKY THE GHOST

The old Hensingersville Hotel, at the corner of Mountain Road and Hensingersville Road, was a wayside watering hole in the area for nearly two centuries.

Horses, wagons and then automobiles would pull up to the handsome, old inn near Alburtis and partake of the keepers' refreshments.

In its last years as a functioning public house, it was more a tavern than a hotel, and has since been transformed into a private residence.

For a long time, though, talk over the bar and across the tables at the Hensingersville Hotel has often centered around its ghost.

At the time of this writing, Maryann Shoemaker owned the property, and the old place was quite familiar to her.

Maryann had lived just down the road from the hotel before she and her husband purchased it. They would amble up to the hotel when Woody and Miriam Grimes ran the bar there.

And, they would hear the tales of "Bucky."

They said Bucky was the name of a prior owner who had taken his own life in the building, and his spirit remained within its walls.

"I didn't believe in ghosts," Maryann affirmed. "But you know, Woody and Miriam would tell about their ghost. They'd constantly say things would happen in that one room. I didn't pay any attention because I didn't believe.

"They sold the place to another lady, and then that lady would talk about things going on in this building. She lived here long. So, she was telling stories, also. I didn't believe her, either!"

But, in 1976, when Maryann and her husband bought the place from that last innkeeper, her attitude toward the supernatural began to change.

"A short time after we bought it," she continued, "things started to happen.

"One night, I was down here tending bar and it was about two in the morning. I was down to one customer. My husband was working third shift at another job, and all of a sudden a door went...like you'd hear in a haunted house. You know, when a squeaky door opens.

"I looked at that last customer, who happened to be our paper delivery man. I asked him if he had heard it. He said he did, and it sounded like a door opening.

"I was worried, because I had four kids sleeping upstairs. It had been very busy earlier that night, and I wondered if somebody might have slipped upstairs.

"I said to him, 'will you stay here until I run upstairs and check everything out?' He said 'sure.'

"I was sure that there was no door in our house that would make a noise like that, none! I came back down, and we talked about it."

Her lone customer suggested he check the outside of the building to make her feel better. The man walked around the property, and found nothing.

Maryann was genuinely frightened. So much so that she called her husband at his job and asked him to come home, truly believing someone was inside their house and business.

He obliged. After a thorough check, nothing, and nobody was found.

Strange occurrences continued to vex the Shoemaker family.

Breakfast at their house was a quick in-and-out situation with their teenage children. They breezed through the kitchen in the morning, almost never eating much of a substantive morning meal.

That's why another episode one morning baffled Maryann. "The kids had gone off to school and I ran down to the drug store for my morning coffee before I would come in and open the bar.

"So, I was gone about an hour, and I came back. There was my frying pan on the stove, and the stove was turned on. Now, my kids couldn't have done that. No way. I was gone about an hour, so that could have caused a lot of damage, you know, with a gas burner. That frying pan was hot. No explanation."

Such aberrations in the kitchen were not uncommon. "The woman who owned the house before us told us she came down one morning and the coffee was perking. She hadn't put it on, but there it was, perking away."

One of the most confounding things to happen to the Shoemakers was the time an hour was stolen from them, presumably by "Bucky."

"One morning we woke up, and the clocks were turned back exactly one hour," she said. "We had a battery-operated clock in our living room and even that was back one hour, so it wasn't electrical."

Unexplainable phenomena continued to confuse Maryann Shoemaker as she carried on business in the tavern below her family's living quarters.

"We had two lights over the bar, one on either end of the bar, and all of a sudden one night, water kept coming out of one of them. I said, 'Oh, my God, now what should I do?' I had three customers at the bar. One of them grabbed a glass and put it under the light. It was catching the water.

"Meanwhile, I ran upstairs. There was nobody home, and my son's bedroom was directly over that light. There was no plumbing up there, no pipes nearby."

The water caused no visible damage to any plaster on the ceiling, and although filling rapidly with water, the light continued to burn brightly.

"There was no explanation for that," Maryann said.

The customers at the bar witnessed the strange occurrence. "This one man was all beside himself," Maryann recalled. "Afterward, he would not sit at that spot anymore. He always sat at the other end of the bar. He's a true believer! I still don't believe it, though. I have to see a ghost to believe."

Maryann may never actually witness an apparition, but continued unexplainable activity in her home and business has baffled her and others.

A toilet fixture, firmly rooted on a cement floor downstairs, often shook as patrons availed themselves of its convenience.

Video machines and juke boxes started up on their own, and one patron reported that a cigarette seemed to be spinning in an ash tray as if turned by an unseen force. On occasion, dishes fell from cupboard shelves.

One time, Maryann went into the basement to pick up a bottle of liquor when, as she recalled, "All of a sudden, I saw a light come on out of the corner of my eye. I looked over and there was a light. It came on by itself. We were here a couple of months, and I didn't know that light bulb was even over in that corner. I went over and pulled the chain, and turned it off and went upstairs in a hurry."

Her husband came home later that day, and she

told him of her weird experience with the basement light. He was concerned, and asked her to show him which light was possibly out of order.

"I took him down and showed him the light. I went to pull it on, and it didn't come on. Never did."

In the mid 1980s, the Shoemakers closed the bar but continued to reside in the old hotel.

"I can't remember who," Maryann said, "but about that time, somebody who was a strong believer in ghosts said to me that the next time anything happened, I should just say, 'In the name of the Father, the Son and the Holy Ghost, what dost thou want?'

"I was in the basement one day, and I heard a noise. Well, those words just came out of my mouth, and I haven't heard a thing since!"

•

Stories about the Eternal Hunter, seem to surface in any region with better than average hunting grounds.

The Lehigh Valley, of course, fits into that category, and there is at least one story about a hunter who has been doomed to roam the forests for an eternity for one reason or another.

In the Blue Mountains, north of Slatedale, the ghostly Eternal Hunter (or, in Pennsylvania German, "Eewich Yaeger") can be heard and sometimes seen in the woods.

They say he shot and wounded a deer very long ago. As he was following the trail of blood to fire the fatal shot, he died in the woods. He will forever pursue his prey.

CHARLIE APPLE

The Brown family got more than it bargained for when they bought the old house along Trexler Blvd. in Allentown.

They got a fine place to raise their children from infancy to adulthood.

They got a stately home which had served as the focal point of a farmstead for nearly a century and a half. Its stone foundation walls were more than a foot thick, and the rooms were copious and comfortable.

A previous owner, Charlie Apple, had made an addition to the old farmhouse in 1948, and the Browns often get the distinct feeling that old Charlie liked the place so much he never really left.

Jim Brown, a Lehigh Valley attorney, is skeptical. As for his wife, Jean, and their children Sarah and Jim III, all are quite convinced that something quite untoward is going on within the walls of their otherwise happy home.

And, whenever there's a bump in the night, a chill in the air or an unseen force over the shoulder,

"Charlie Apple" is given the credit, or the blame!

Jean Brown says Charlie was in his sixties when he died in the house after being bedridden for a long time.

"When we'd hear noises or anything happened, we'd always say, 'Charlie Apple's acting up again,'" Jean Brown affirms.

The Browns have resided in the old farmhouse for more than 30 years.

"It was worse when the kids were smaller," she says. "They're all grown up and out of the house now. It seemed like there was more activity going on then. Little things would happen.

"Friends would come, they'd be upstairs and they'd say they'd hear somebody come up. Some of them wouldn't even visit any more."

Jean Brown recalls times when certain very confined spots in the house would turn icy cold, when doors would open on their own, and when strange figures were seen in both the old and new sections of the house.

"At night, I would close our closet door upstairs," she recalls, "and it would click shut. It always used to be open in the morning. We'd take special care to close the door, and it would always be open.

"Also in the bathroom, I'd get up in the morning and that door would be open. When I'd go to bed at night, I was sure it was closed."

Lehigh Valley Ghost Stories

There were trifle, but baffling incidents. "I'd hear a lot of noises like walking, and sometimes I would feel like someone came in and lay right beside me in the bedroom. I could feel somebody beside me, but nobody was. It scared me half to death," Jean says.

"I don't sleep up there. It's just those little things that happen, like somebody's walking or scurrying here and there. You can feel the coldness. You can feel him go by. Occasionally, I'd get the faint smell of cologne, too."

But nothing was as disturbing to Jean as something which took place shortly after her father passed on.

There was a picture of her father on Jean's wall. Following his death, those picture was turned around, face to the wall!

"My dad wasn't facing us, he was facing the wall," Jean shrugs. "It was turned backwards, turned completely around. Two times it was like that!"

Jean suspected someone in the family was responsible for the turning of the picture. "Everyone denied it," she says.

While Jim Brown, the father, is not thoroughly convinced that whatever happens in the home is of a ghostly origin, Jim Brown, the son, is on his mother's side.

"Yes," he says, "we'd hear the basic noises. Doors that are locked at night and open in the morning, things like that."

The younger Mr. Brown, a Kutztown University student at the time of this writing, has had even more frightening experiences than his mother.

"I had two, uh, appearances," he reveals. "I talked to two other people who have had similar experiences in the house."

Jim's visions came in the old part of the house, in an upstairs bedroom, not too long ago. Those apparitions, however, seem to fly in the face of the "Charlie Apple" theory.

"It was a woman," he says. It seemed to appear quietly, take shape, and then slowly fade away.

He says he has felt a presence peering over the foot of his bed, and has felt the cold spots in the house.

"One of my friends, Bob Cawley," Jim says, "also came upstairs once and saw a figure he couldn't explain. Now he refuses to go into that house at all."

•

SPOOKS
AND BOOKS
The Haunting of the
Easton Public Library

If any building *looked* haunted, it's the Easton Public Library.

Completed in 1903 and fashioned in a classic Victorian style, the library building, tucked into a tree-shaded corner of town at Sixth and Church Streets, has the classic lines of a place which would harbor many tales of intrigue, mystery and romance.

Indeed it does. After all, it is a library.

But the tales of mystery and imagination within its hallowed walls are not only within the pages of its thousands of books.

They say the old library is haunted, and wait until you hear how!

Around the turn of the century, the plot upon which the library was to be built was overgrown with vines, thick underbrush and trees. It was a monumental task just to clear the site for the construction job.

One day, as workmen were uprooting the bushes

and brush, they uprooted something quite unexpected.

As they dug to dislodge the deep tangles in the soil, they came upon a grave. No one had known it was there.

Human bones, skulls and tattered clothing marked what was intended to be the the final resting place of some anonymous being.

The digging continued, and one by one, more graves were found. When the rotting coffins and skeletons were counted, more than 500 burials were confirmed on the site.

Among those who were interred in the old graveyard were the noteworthy and the nameless.

William Parsons, who is credited with being one of the surveyors who laid out the city of Easton, was afforded a re-burial in an honored location near the entrance to the library.

Elizabeth Bell ("Mammy") Morgan, a Quaker who fled the yellow fever epidemic in Philadelphia in the late 1700s, was also buried in the lost cemetery. When her remains were found, she was reinterred on the library grounds and her grave was marked by an ancient Indian grindstone placed by the Northampton County Historical and Genealogical Society.

Best known for her commodious hotel in Williams Township and her knowledge of the law, Mrs. Morgan was quite the character in life.

Some believe she may be quite the character even today, nearly two centuries after she departed her earthly existence!

While "Mammy" Morgan's bones were given a more proper burial at the library, it is said that her restless spirit still glides among the stacks and shelves of the old library.

Over the years, several patrons, passersby and professionals in the library have reported seeing or sensing a woman's ghostly countenance. Those who knew of Mammy Morgan claimed it was she, wandering within and through the library walls.

Moreover, any ghostly presences on the library grounds may well be attributed to any number of disembodied entities.

Indeed, a persistent legend around Easton has it that there were reports of ghostly lights and sights being seen in the old graveyard from the very moment it was cleared for the library construction.

Perhaps a bizarre incident in that clearing and construction project supports the concept that energy could well swirl in the area, thus stirring supernatural occurrences.

The fates of the Morgan and Parsons bones is one story. What happened to 30 other individuals who were ostensibly resting in peace on the grounds is something else altogether.

As construction of the library proceeded, most of the decomposed corpses were identified, claimed by relatives, and moved to more permanent plots.

Thirty bodies, or what was left of them, were

unidentified and unclaimed. The remains, often merely a collection of random bones and unmatched skulls, were somewhat unceremoniously buried in a mass grave.

In an almost hideous and perhaps hasty move, workers gathered the dry bones, the splintered coffins, and random bits and pieces of lost lives and placed them in the deep pit.

Over ensuing decades, however, the earthen fill over the mass grave settled, and resulted in a slight but noticeable depression in the ground surface near the northeastern exit of the library grounds.

This grisly landmark loomed for many years as a reminder to all who toiled at the library that they did so on the site of an old graveyard, and next to the common grave of unknown dead.

With these ominous signs all around (and under) them, employees of the library have been wary of the possible consequences.

In and out of second-floor offices, library workers have seen and heard strange things.

Filing cabinets slowly rolled open on their own, doors which were definitely locked by custodians just hours before creaked open, and at least one employee felt the very distinct stroke of a hand across her hair as she worked on the mezzanine level.

Despite the eerie silence of any library, the almost Gothic setting of the Easton Area Public Library, and the inarguable fact that the building is set on an old graveyard, those who work there tend to maintain a level of nonchalance toward the notion of ghosts wandering in their midst.

One librarian totally shrugged off the possibility that Mammy Morgan's or anyone else's ghost rises from a grave and takes nocturnal strolls in and around the library.

"The only ghosts in here," she said, "are in the stories in those old books."

Maybe so, ma'am.

Maybe not.

•

Sometimes, the best-laid plans of powwowers go astray.

When told by a Lehigh County farmer that his cows give only bloody milk, a powwower suggested the cure be to place fresh cow dung in a crock, seal it, and bake it.

Thus, the evil spirits would be cast out of the cow, and it would give good milk.

The farmer followed the powwower's advice, but he left the concoction in the oven too long. The crock exploded, the oven door blew out, and baked cow dung was splattered all over the room!

Lehigh Valley Ghost Stories

HANGMAN'S
ISLAND

A small island in the Delaware River near its confluence with the Bushkill Creek has been known as Getter's Island for more than a century and a half.

Just who "Getter" was, how the island came to be named after him, and how his presence may well still be with us is an interesting story.

It was February 28, 1833 when the battered body of Margaret Getter was discovered in a quarry near Easton. Investigators determined she had been strangled.

Suspicions led directly to the woman's husband, Charles.

All who knew the Getters knew that all was not well. The marriage was forced by Margaret's pregnancy, and for the approximately thirty stormy days they were married, Charles Getter was brutal, and on more than one occasion made it clear to witnesses that someday he would get her, and the unwanted child, out of his life forever.

Lehigh Valley Ghost Stories

Getter's apprehension and trial gripped Northampton County for nearly eight months. After a bitter court battle, Getter was found guilty, and sentenced to be hanged by the neck until dead.

His execution was set for October 4, 1833, and when word of the pending hanging spread around town, officials quickly realized the grisly hanging would draw a massive crowd of morbid thrill-seekers.

Executions were held in full view of the public in those days, usually in the town squares.

In Easton at the time, that ground upon which the gallows was built was called The Great Square. It is known today as Centre Square.

For whatever reason, though, Charles Getter's execution was moved to a small island in the Delaware River. It is theorized that the island vantage point was more desirable since more spectators could gawk at the hanging from the river banks.

Early the morning of October 4, Getter was led from his cell across a flotilla of small boats which were lashed together to form an impromptu bridge to the island.

As a hush fell over the onlooking crowds, the hangman fitted the noose over Getter's shrouded head.

Admitting nothing and expressing no remorse, Getter nodded to continue the procedure which would lead to his death.

The Northampton County sheriff checked his knife. It was razor-sharp, and would easily slash the

50

rope and send Getter into eternity.

With an anguished motion, the sheriff cut the rope and Getter's body was sent dangling. He twisted, gagged, and choked for only seconds when the rope supporting him snapped. Still alive, but in agony, Getter fell to the floor of the gallows.

Getter doubtlessly smirked inside the black hood which covered his face. He had defied the hangman, he thought.

Determined to carry out the death sentence, the executioner summoned more sturdy rope. Twenty minutes later, another noose was fashioned, slipped over Getter's head, and the procedure was repeated.

That time, Getter was held firm. His neck was crushed, his wreathing and wriggling ceased quickly, and with a wrenching hack, the last breath was squeezed from his throat.

Not long after the murderer's body was removed from the little rise of land in the Delaware, the island became known as Getter's Island.

To this day, it is said that the ghost of old Charles Getter still inhabits the island.

An old tale in Easton has it that if you look upon the island and ask Getter to explain why he murdered his wife, the voice of his spirit will echo a mysterious answer.

Moreover, poor Margaret Getter's ghost supposedly remains earthbound, and can be seen in the vicinity of the Northampton County Country Club, along the William Penn Highway.

She is said to be dressed in a long, black dress and a black bonnet. Her eyes are fixed in an eternal stare. If approached and spoken to, she will not reply. She will brush by, leaving an icy chill in her wake, and vanish.

•

"From 1963 to 1975, my family and I lived in a house on Main Street in Hellertown.

"One night, my mother nearly leaped from one of the bedroom windows and on another occasion, my pet died gruesomely under unusual circumstances.

"While living there, we were plagues by slugs. On slug even crawled into our kitchen. I dreamed about a slug the night before my pet was killed.

"On one occasion, a bolt of lighting shot through the kitchen window and struck the light fixture. On another, I dreamed the night prior I would be struck by a bolt of lightning. That dream saved my life the next day when the even actually occurred, as I remembered the dream just in time to spare my life.

"Once, a minister's wife gasped that we should leave the house because she felt an evil presence. She died prematurely.

"Another family that moved there after we left experienced weird things, too.

"It all sound like something from Stephen King, but it's all real."

Michele D. Fehr

THE GHOST OF
THE STATE THEATRE

W hen the sets are struck, the lights go dark, and silence casts an eerie calm, does a benevolent phantom wander within the cavernous confines of the historic State Theatre in Easton?

Some say yes, and some believe they know the identity of the ghost.

They call him Fred.

The bright spot in the heart of downtown Easton, the theater traces its origins to 1873, when the spacious, handsome Northampton National Bank was built on the site of the present State.

In a sweeping renovation of the property in 1910, the first theater was established. Owned by and named after John Neumoyer, the 500-seat vaudeville house presented top acts, booked by the Circle Theatres group of New York City.

As the sun began to set on vaudeville and motion pictures shone brightly as the entertainment trend of the future, the Neumoyer briefly became the Northampton Street Theatre, and then the Colonial.

Lehigh Valley Ghost Stories

From 1914 to 1925, moviegoers plunked down a nickel for matinees and a dime after dark and enjoyed the latest films.

In 1925, the Wilmer and Vincent Amusement Co. decided to transform the theater into a showplace its architect claimed would dazzle the local citizenry.

As gold leaf appointments were applied to the vaulted ceiling, gilded frescoes and plaster relief friezes were crafted into the walls, artisans labored to fulfill the designer's promise.

No expense was spared as top decorators were employed and a full $400,000 was budgeted to provide all the creature comforts for performers and patrons alike.

Re-named the State and placed on the legendary Keith Vaudeville circuit, the spectacular new theater opened on March 8, 1926 to an enthusiastic audience of nearly 2,000. Each was, indeed, dazzled.

World-class live acts, newsreels and two-reeler silents gave way to talkies, and by the mid-1930s, the transition was nearly complete. The State was purchased by the New Jersey-based Fabian Theaters, and thrived as a movie house.

Just as vaudeville gave way to silents, and silents to talkies, the motion picture became threatened by television.

From the 1950s through 1980, the State's respectability went into a freefall. Gutted of the technical marvels which made it the darling of vaudevillians, there were symptoms that the theater was suffering a slow, agonizing death.

Ever so briefly, it became a porno palace, then a raucous rock house. In the hands of absentee and inconsiderate owners, the State suffered indignity on top of indignity until 1980, when it unceremoniously closed and faced near certain demolition.

A public and private partnership rallied to raise the community's awareness and then the money needed to pump new life into the decrepit downtown derelict.

On December 8, 1989, the fruits of that partnership's labors were savored as the magnificent "new" State Theatre was re-dedicated with top name acts and a champagne reception.

Fred, the resident ghost, couldn't have been happier that night.

Through some of the most challenging years of the State Theatre's existence, one man, J. Fred Osterstock, reigned supreme as manager of the facility.

It is his spirit, many believe, which haunts the State.

"Have I seen Fred? No," says one person who has participated in many events at the theater. He continues, "Have I felt Fred's presence? Oh, yes. Very much so!"

The middle-aged performer and volunteer says there is a feeling which permeates the old theater, and it sometimes manifests itself in mysterious ways.

"About all I can tell you about any personal experiences I have had is the one time I was standing in the front lobby, all alone...I thought...when there was a pinpoint of light on the floor. It couldn't have been more than an inch in diameter.

"I glanced down at it, and it seemed to move slowly across the floor. I looked up to find its source, and could trace it to nothing.

"I placed my hand above it, trying to block it out and find out where it was coming from. Now, this is weird, but you have to believe me. It was definitely a light on the floor, as if someone was shining a small flashlight there. I had no doubt about it.

"But, when I blocked it with my hand, it remained on the floor. In fact, I tried moving my hand all around it to block its source, but it remained light.

"Now, this only took a few seconds, you know, but it was strange. The strangest thing is when I tried to actually cup my hand over the light to, well, capture it. Just as I kneeled down to do that, and got my hands over the light, it actually slid across the floor, very slowly.

"I backed off. I probably looked silly, but unfortunately, or maybe *fortunately*, there was nobody there to witness what was going on.

"Anyway, this light moved across the floor slowly at first, and I still couldn't find its source. Then, in a flash, it slid into a corner, and up a wall. After that, it just disappeared. I guessed I was just seeing things, or going nuts.

"Or, maybe it was Fred, playing a trick on me!"

Fred is not so much the trickster, but more the quiet, unthreatening type whose ghost seems to be just out of reach, just out of sight.

"Oh, yes, Fred's here," said another theater worker. "His spirit is throughout this place. Usually, he's just around the next corner, or just beyond the shadows. If something happens, good or bad, Fred is either blamed or credited. He's very much at home here, and we have no problem with him."

Osterstock managed the State for thirty years starting in 1926, and was said to be a hard taskmaster.

In his last year at the helm of the facility, he actually lived in the office just above the foyer.

While many theaters have "unofficial" ghosts who play pranks on actors and stage crew members, Fred has almost been sanctioned by the theater's management.

In the handsome program book which was distributed at the re-dedication of the theater in 1989, a full page was dedicated to Fred, the former manager and Fred, the ghost.

The article detailed the experience of as many as a half-dozen people, including members of the theater's board of directors, who reported having encounters with the spirit.

One individual, Ken Klabunde, provided an eerie

account of a night he was alone, closing the theater, when he noticed a figure on an otherwise empty stage. He looked at the unknown person closely enough to discern facial features, but could not wend his way to the stage quickly enough to approach the individual.

In fact, as he was walking toward the stage, the figure vanished.

Several weeks later, while rummaging through documents and photographs related to the theater, he came across a picture of a distinguished gentleman. The picture was that of J. Fred Osterstock, the former theater manager, who had been dead many, many years.

Klabunde knew, though, that the face on that photograph was the same as the face on the man who left the stage that night and disappeared into the darkened auditorium.

It was Fred, the ghost of the State Theatre.

•

AN APPARITION
IN EAST TEXAS

The suburbs of Allentown have stretched into the little Lower Macungie Township town of East Texas these days, but there was a time when the village was a remote and quiet place.

Quiet, that is, except for the traffic which has always passed through it for one or more reasons.

Years ago, much of that traffic was generated by the many nearby iron mines.

Legend has it that along one lane just outside of town, Minesite Road, a wandering ghost once caused havoc with passing horse riders and wagon drivers.

The ghost was that of a man who hanged himself along the road, and was doomed to haunt the site forever. The details of the story, and the isolation of Minesite Road, have been lost in time.

A more vivid tale of a haunting in East Texas comes from a very well-known woman, indeed one of the most respected residents of the town. Because of her illustrious career and her personal associations, she asked that her real name not be used in this story. Let us call her Dorothy.

The house in which Dorothy and her family lived is in the heart of East Texas, and has been renovated and altered in recent years.

But any architectural alterations could not dispel the memories Dorothy has kept within her of family life in the old place.

"The dining room had a huge walk-in fireplace when we lived there," the woman recalled as she detailed some of the unexplained incidents which took place there.

"Often times in the morning when we came down the steps, we'd swear that someone was baking bread. It smelled so strong, and it would be so delightful. I'd expect to come out in the dining room and find a loaf of fresh bread on the table. That was one thing, and it happened frequently.

"On the cellar door, which was also in that dining room, there was one of those old lift-up latches. We'd be sitting in the living room watching TV, and we'd just hear somebody coming up the steps. We'd hear the latch rattle. It would be like somebody slammed the door, but the door never opened.

"We'd hear sounds. And in my daughter's bedroom, she often, through the night, would hear somebody pacing back and forth. She was about 16 or 17 at the time."

The woman, who lived with her family in the

house in the middle of East Texas for five years, continued that some of the experiences were more spooky than others.

"One night when my daughter wasn't home," she continued, "I woke up and I heard somebody call out very clearly. *Very* clearly. I thought my daughter had come home, but there was nobody there.

"My husband woke up several times through the night and would think my daughter was standing by the bed, when in reality she was in her own bed. I never saw anything, but he claimed he definitely saw somebody standing there.

"And, our dog at the time would sit and watch, as if she was watching somebody walking. Then, she would cock her head like someone was talking to her. You know, she'd just have a real attentive look on her face. She'd just be staring into nothing, really."

The family members never felt threatened by the mysterious sights and sounds. "It never seemed malicious," she continued. "It never seemed that it was going to hurt anybody."

"Besides," she added, "these things happened to frequently, really, that you kind of got used to it."

There was one episode, however, which did have more impact on the family.

"The one thing that did kind of shake us up a little was the time our daughter was recording albums into a portable cassette recorder using a free-standing microphone.

"Later on, we played the tape back, and after the music ended, there was a real high-pitched sound like feedback. We just kind of looked at each other. Then, all of a sudden, you just heard this very distinctly: 'HELP ME!' That, we didn't like too much. She destroyed the tape. That shook her up, but it was very real. It was like a whisper, but very clear...'HELP ME...'

"That really made the hair stand up on the back of the neck! That was the only thing I would say annoyed us. It was also just before we moved out."

Despite her brushes with the supernatural, the woman remains somewhat the skeptic.

"Let's put it this way, I have an open mind. I was raised in the Pennsylvania Dutch influence. I went to pow-wows. I was born in Wescosville. Just because you don't understand something doesn't mean it isn't there."

•

KEEPING THE GHOSTS HAPPY

Just south of Hellertown, where Route 412, Leithsville Road, meets Flint Hill Road, is the ancient Leithsville Inn.

Its current proprietor, Adrian Sinko, boasts on his business card that his place is known for its food...and its spirits.

For purely business purposes, "spirits" in this case refers to alcoholic beverages. For the purposes of this book, the word takes on an entirely different meaning.

They say the Leithsville Inn is haunted. And Adrian Sinko takes that possibility very seriously.

The building dates to the time the Leith brothers settled there, and was a wayside tavern when the Liberty Bell was smuggled out of Philadelphia for safe-keeping in Allentown during the Revolutionary War. The wagons which lugged the bell "up country" may well have passed by the inn, and its teamsters may well have stopped by for some refreshments.

All of that is historical speculation. And, for the most part, the notion that the Leithsville Inn is haunted remains largely unconfirmed.

But don't try to tell that to Mr. Sinko.

"The garage across the street used to be stables," he said. "When we first moved in, in the early 1980s, a lot of people told us that there are ghosts in here."

There is little documentation to that effect, but there is much in the way of legend to support the proposition.

"I really can't tell you much," Sinko continued. "Someone was killed in here, or something like that. And, they took him out to be hanged or something like that."

Something like that.

Longtime neighbors do attest to the telling and re-telling of the Leithsville legend.

It seems there were once orchards virtually surrounding the old inn. It is believed that whoever haunts the place may have been involved in an 18th century crime, and was dragged from the premises, declaring his innocence. Mob rule prevailed, however, and the hapless gent was lynched somewhere on the property.

The tale smacks of a more familiar story in Jim Thorpe, Carbon County, where the hand print of a condemned member of the ruthless Mollie Maguires who was dragged from his cell to the gallows has never disappeared.

That convicted "Mollie" tried to prevent his

jailers from pulling him from his cell by placing his arm on the wall and holding on for dear life, proclaiming that he was innocent. He vowed that his hand print would never be scrubbed from the wall, proving they were executing the wrong man.

The man was executed, the hand print remains indelible on a Carbon County Jail wall.

Adrian has heard that there is such an inexpungeable hand print on a wall in an upstairs room at his inn.

"I'll never get to it," he said, "because the walls are paneled today."

Oh, he *could* get to it if he really wanted to. But perhaps he really doesn't want to tempt fate.

Adrian admits he has made certain concessions to whatever may or may not haunt the Leithsville Inn.

"The big joke around here is why does Adrian keep the televisions on when there's nobody home.

"I always say it's to keep the ghosts happy, and give them something to do so they don't bother us!"

Adrian had better hope the ghosts can tolerate the re-run season!

•

THEY CALL THE GHOST "BEETHOVEN"

Is there more than melodious camaraderie within the walls of the Beethoven Waldheim just south of Leithsville, in the southern corner of Northampton County?

The handsome Waldheim is really the 1738 stone bank barn built by John Leith, and was the homestead of the family which gave the nearby crossroads village its name.

Today, the barn is the centerpiece of a complex which includes a dining room, kitchen and rathskeller bar.

Set on 27 wooded acres drained by a small stream, the building is the home of the storied Beethoven Choruses.

Those singing groups include what was founded in 1891 as the Beethoven Maennerchor (an all-male chorus) and the 1922 Beethoven Damenchor (all-female).

The award-winning choirs trace their roots to the musical city of Bethlehem, and their Germanic repertoire has pleased the ears of audiences around the world.

The singing club expanded the old Leith barn in 1962, and use it as a clubhouse, rehearsal and concert hall.

But, certain ethereal elements within the walls of the big barn may provide their own kinds of shows after the last note is sung and the last singer has gone home.

Connected to the singing club is a social club, a members-only lounge.

Lois Black is a member of the board of directors of that social club, and she confirmed widespread rumors that the barn is haunted.

"I really don't pay much attention to it anymore," Lois said of the possibility. "When I come in and I'm by myself, I just accept it," she affirmed.

While she has never really seen anything (as others say they have), she certainly has heard what could only be described as "mysterious" sounds, mostly upstairs.

Anna Eichlin has heard the sounds, too. A cook and cleaning lady at the lounge, Anna added that the ghost is particularly feisty when her boss's wife is around.

That boss is caterer Bruce Miniarik, and he agreed with Anna's assessment.

Anna detailed the reasons she felt the spirit may have it out for Susan Miniarik.

Lehigh Valley Ghost Stories

"When she first started working in here," she said, "there was a light fixture. She was standing under it, and the thing fell.

"Then, about two years later, she happened to be in the kitchen, talking to me. She was saying something to me, and that same light fixture fell."

Fairly flimsy stuff to qualify as "ghostly," perhaps. But it gets better.

"I'd go in at five in the morning," Anna continued, "and I'd hear something like somebody walking up the stairs. That didn't bother me, because it's an old building, and it creaks.

"Another time, Bruce sent me upstairs in the dark to get something, and all of a sudden the whole place got cold. I turned around, and saw this *black thing*, well, just sort of *take off!*"

With that, Anna bolted downstairs to tell Bruce. "He said 'whoo-ee-oo, it's only Beethoven, coming to get you!'"

At the time, under the circumstances, Anna didn't appreciate her boss's humor.

"There's got to be a ghost in here," Anna concluded. "You hear things...you hear things. You hear chairs moving. And, you *know* you're the only one in the building at five in the morning.

"I had Susan so flipped out, she's scared to leave me here alone. I said, look, it won't harm me!"

Anna deals with the disembodied sounds and occasional apparition with firmness. "I just tell him to

68

get lost...go away...I have work to do!," she chuckled.

Other than that strange *black thing* Anna Eichlin said she saw, there have been few visual contacts with the ghost they've come to call "Beethoven."

"I believe in ghosts," she said. "They're around somewhere. I don't know that you can see one, though. Maybe just shadows. You can't really see a human figure or anything."

As for Bruce Miniarik, his own experiences certainly contribute to the notion that there is a ghost in the Waldheim.

"I don't know if they're actual experiences, or just my imagination," said the caterer.

"It's always been a kind of joke around here, you know, that the place is haunted...that it's got a ghost and all that," he continued.

Still, some incidents which have unfolded before his eyes have left him wondering.

"I know that a while back, once in a while I would be in the kitchen here working, and I would turn around, knowing I had every burner on the stove turned off, and one or two of them would be on.

"And, we had these ceiling lights in the kitchen. Twice, this happened to my wife, and it's weird. We were working here, and she was waitressing and standing right underneath one of the lights.

"She turned around and took two steps out of place, and the globe of the light dropped right on the floor. If she'd not taken those two steps away, she'd have been hit right on the head!

"But the thing that was really weird was, a couple years later, she came over here one morning after church with the kids and was standing in the kitchen talking to me and the *exact same thing happened!*

"We made a joke about it, that the ghost didn't like her at all. It never happened to anyone else here."

Bruce confirmed that the old barn can give one the willies at times.

"At night, when you're here by yourself, or when there are only one or two people in the place, you know you hear some strange noises, like somebody's walking across the floor upstairs.

"Of course, it's an old building, so it could just be heaving or something."

...or something else!

•

Beware of the ghost of a young woman said to walk boldly down Hamilton Street near Hess's Department Store.

An Allentown police officer who wishes to remain anonymous, says the ghostly figure is that of a girl who was struck and killed by a car many years ago. He says he has seen the figure late at night, on the curb, staring blankly into the street on which she died.

THE GHOSTS OF
HAWK MOUNTAIN

No place in the greater Lehigh Valley can boast more natural beauty than the lofty peaks of Hawk Mountain.

Although the Hawk Mountain Sanctuary, a premiere nature center and world-renown refuge for birds of prey, straddles Berks and Schuylkill Counties, it is situated just over the Lehigh County line. And indeed, the impact of the ghostly tales which emanate from its wooded depths stretches well beyond its boundaries.

While Hawk Mountain, and the valleys which spread before it, is certainly a showplace of natural splendor, it is also abundant in wild and chilling stories of the *super*natural.

It is, quite simply, one of the most haunted areas in the United States of America.

This is no idle boast. In fact, those who live and work on the mountain certainly wish it were not so blessed, or cursed, with the level of activity--the spiral of energy--which swirls throughout its trees, trails,

71

rocks and ridges.

"I don't want to believe too strongly in this stuff," says sanctuary curator Jim Brett, "because I never want to leave this wonderful mountain."

The "stuff" to which the hardy man of the mountain refers to are the many confirmed and documented encounters many people have had with the phantoms that stalk that "wonderful mountain."

The legends of Hawk Mountain are rooted deeply in dark and distant times before the first white man set foot on the rock-strewn slopes of the foreboding hill.

What the natives who populated the region centuries ago might have called the mountain has been lost in time and translations.

What they felt about it, however, is fairly well researched.

To the Lenni Lenape Indians, it harbored a certain sanctity. Nudging higher than the hills around it, it was close to their gods. Therefore, it was the site of ceremonies and rituals.

Archaeological evidence has been found to verify this, and the deep attachment the Indians had to the mountain may well have been the spiritual spark which ignited the almost demonic flames which cast their frightening glow on all who seek the Hawk Mountain which is somewhere beyond the realm of the known.

What is known about the earliest recorded

history of what is now called Hawk Mountain is that it was the site of a tragedy in 1756, a tragedy which is the first link in a chain of bizarre incidents which pepper the history of the hill.

As white settlers ventured into the foothills of the Blue Mountains in the mid-18th century, the natives tried to tolerate the incursion. Treaties were made, treaties were broken, and that tolerance was weakened as the Indians were forced deeper into the the forests, away from the fertile soil of the valleys.

Determined to conquer what was then the American frontier, the settlers built a chain of forts along the base of the mountains, through Berks, Lehigh and Northampton counties, and sought to protect the homesteaders.

The Indians' frustrations built to a fever's pitch, and attack followed attack in farmhouses across the lowlands. The historical references of Indian raids in the area are simple, but sobering, as recorded. A brief sampling:

•February, 1756: George Zeisloff and wife, two boys and a girl, murdered

•June, 1757: Adam Trump, found with a knife and a spear (fixed to a pole four feet long) in his body

•July, 1757: Martin Jaeger and wife,

murdered. Abraham Sechler's wife, and a
child of Adam Clauss were scalped at the
same time

•September, 1757: A man shot in bed
whilst sick

One of the most gruesome attacks to take place
on or near Hawk Mountain was in 1756.

In February of that year, all but one member of
the Gerhardt family were slaughtered by Indians. The
only survivor, eleven-year old Jacob, watched from
behind nearby bushes as his father was called out of
the family' small cabin, and was hacked to death.

The home was set ablaze, and Jacob watched in
horror as his mother and five brothers and sisters
were incinerated.

A mature Jacob Gerhardt returned to the
mountain in 1793, after a permanent peace with the
Indians had been established. He built a more
substantial "cottage" near the top of the 1,500-foot
mountain, and the property remained in his and his
heirs' names for six decades.

The next property owners of record were
George and Priscilla Bolich, who resided there for 52
years, eventually selling the land to Margaret and
Matthias Schambacher.

It is the Schambacher era in which history and

mystery begin to mingle on Hawk Mountain.

Matthias Schambacher (or "Schaumboch," as it is spelled in some references) transformed the old Gerhardt stone home into a kind of wayside tavern, making and selling applejack and Blue Mountain tea to travelers who used the road over the mountain as a crude, steep shortcut from the lower coal regions to the Lehigh Valley.

Most of these travelers included peddlers and deliverymen who would be anxious to stop at Schambacher's Tavern for refreshment.

Ostensibly, they would pull up, secure their horses and carriages, amble into Matthias' place, have a drink or two, and be on their way.

The trouble is, some of them never made it to where they were heading.

One by one, men disappeared from that lonely road up over the mountain. The last place they could possibly have been seen would have been Schambacher's Tavern.

Two, then four, then eight, then a dozen...these wagon drivers simply vanished without a trace. That is, until something very strange happened.

It is recorded that Matthias Schambacher was seen wearing and selling surplus and used Civil War uniforms just weeks after a used Civil War uniform peddler was reported missing somewhere between Kempton and Orwigsburg.

Suspicions began to mount that Schambacher

may have waylaid the man and stolen his cargo.

But, there was only scant evidence. Local residents attempted to question the gruff Schambacher, but were repelled as they approached his property.

Weird reports circulated in the valley below. Some folks told of globs of blood on the dirt road between Schambacher's house and barn. Some told of mournful, moaning sounds coming from the basement of the house. Some told of unexplainable wagon parts hidden near the small barnyard at Schambacher's.

But there was no firm evidence which would link the man with what had become suspected murders.

Schambacher had never been a popular man. Local children were warned to steer clear of him. His secrets were many.

The gravest secrets of all were to eventually be revealed to a startled but somewhat expectant citizenry as Matthias Schambacher lay dying.

Nearly everyone for miles around had become convinced that Schambacher had a hand in the disappearances and assumed deaths of the men.

Thus, it was a grim task for a local minister who was beckoned to Schambacher's side in early March, 1879. Word had gotten to the pastor that Margaret Schambacher had requested his presence because her husband's conditioned had worsened, and he had told her he had something to confess.

Even the most thorough and compassionate psychological and theological training that minister could have received could *not* have prepared him for what he was to hear from the lips of the dying man.

Tales told and retold on the mountain say the conversation went something like this:

"Matthias, why do you call me here?"

"Because, in whatever time I have left on this earth, I must confess my sins."

"And what sins may they be, Matthias?"

"I have taken the lives of men."

"Men, you say? How many men?"

"I know not. I cannot remember. I lost count at fourteen, for only fourteen skulls would fit in my well."

A shocked pastor gulped, regained his composure, and continued:

"And Matthias, how did you kill these men?"

"With my ax."

"And how...where...did you dispose of their remains?"

"I stripped the flesh from the bones, and placed the bones on the rocks for the beasts of the forest to pick clean."

As for the flesh, there is wide and horrid speculation as to how it was used.

In the most grisly speculation of all, it is said that after Matthias Schambacher claimed his first victim, he added fresh sausage to his tavern's menu.

This is only speculation, mind you, but it is the stuff of legend, and no legend anywhere is any more gruesome than the legend of Hawk Mountain, and the role Matthias Schambacher played in it.

From the day of his death to the present, all things of substance left to perpetuate the man's reputation seem to have their own stories attached to them.

The day Schambacher was buried in the graveyard of New Bethel Church near Kempton has gone down in the annals of local lore because of a fearsome phantasmic display which only enriched the legend.

Obviously, Schambacher could not have been among the most popular persons in the area. Fittingly, only his widow, the preacher and the gravedigger were present that day on the windswept cemetery hill.

It is recorded that as Schambacher's coffin was being lowered into the grave, the somber trio was startled as thunder rumbled in the distance.

Their attention turned to Hawk Mountain, the hulk of which formed a wooded wall to the west.

As they cowered in fear and disbelief, deep gray and black clouds tumbled over the mountain, spinning and surging in their direction.

The roar of the thunder was incessant. The sky darkened, casting an eeriness across the graveyard.

At once, with no warning whatsoever, a spear of lightning crashed from the clouds and struck Matthias Schambacher's fresh grave.

Thunder clapped and shook the horrified funeral party to their souls.

Another crack...another flash...another bolt of lightning seemed to take aim on the grave. The three fled for safety, too scared to rationalize what was happening.

The savage storm subsided as suddenly as it started. After assuring each other the occurrences were mere freaks of nature, the confessed killer's corpse was laid to rest in peace.

Or was it?

Some of the old-timers up in that section say screaming and moaning sounds can still be heard, wafting down from the mountains.

One seasoned citizen from the Stony Run area swears what happened to him one day is true.

He was driving a tractor slowly along the road which leads past New Bethel Church and Schambacher's very prominent tombstone, when he was temporarily blinded by a sudden flash of light.

It seemed to illuminate the whole countryside, he says, but centered itself along the road. He slammed on the brakes and pulled to the side of the road slowly. As he regained his senses, and his vision, he was taken by a strange glow moving down the road toward him. It seemed to stand about ten feet tall and moved very slowly. At first, he thought it was a fog, mist or some other earthly phenomenon, but that thought was quickly dashed.

The man saw the glow gradually develop into what he swore was the shape of a man. For a brief moment, he saw arms and legs take definite form. Perhaps two seconds after they formed, the glow vanished into thin air.

The man had not been drinking, nor was he excessively tired. Nor had he ever had any particular belief in, or experience with, ghosts.

To this day, however, his voice quivers as he repeats his story.

Another older farmer from the area was passing by the graveyard one afternoon when he met up with what he could only describe as, in his thick Pennsylvania German dialect, "a schpuk!"

The man was not a believer, and in fact never gave much thought at all to ghosts and "schpuks." What happened to him that day as he drove his old pickup past Schambacher's grave has given him pause for thought.

As he passed the cemetery, he noticed ahead of him a fairly well-dressed old man, walking slowly, with slumped shoulders and a downcast head, in his direction.

In that valley where most folks know most other folks, he took a better look as they drew closer. There was a good chance he'd recognize the walker.

Nature took over for one or two fateful seconds, and the man behind the wheel sneezed. The brief distraction was just long enough to cast the man in utter confusion. As he looked to find and hopefully greet the mysterious pedestrian, he couldn't find him.

Knowing the lay of the land there, he reckoned it would have been virtually impossible for a man to disappear from sight in that short a time.

Dumbfounded, the driver casually glanced in his rear-view mirror and nearly veered off the road. There, walking far behind him, was the same figure he had seen not two seconds before, an equal distance in front of him.

This time, he slowed to a crawl and kept his eyes on the mirror and the man. What he saw tested him. What he saw was the figure grow smaller, second by second. As it seemed to shrink, it also seemed to become more and more transparent, until, as the man explained, "the damned thing just disappeared, right in front of my eyes, and right at the tombstone of Schambacher!"

This writer has had several brushes with the unexplainable at Schambacher's grave, and on Hawk Mountain.

For several years, on Halloween, or on a Friday the 13th (just for the effect), up to 85 people on "Ghost Tours" organized by Macaronis Travel of Reading, have ventured to the mountain.

In chilly darkness or in the moonlit warmth of autumn, we bravely entered the domain of Schambacher, and the other spirits which inhabit the magical mountain.

We have gathered in the commons room which stands on the site of the old Schambacher barn, where

Matthias is said to have carried out his nefarious deeds. There, we have enjoyed light snacks (consumed *before* the details of how the ax murderer disposed of his victims' bodies were revealed), and gathered to hear the stories of those who have experienced the ghosts of Hawk Mountain.

Sanctuary curator Jim Brett and his staff, interns and neighbors have peppered the night with startling special effects, ersatz corpses in borrowed coffins, and realistic rituals played out for the benefit of the visitors.

Gracious for and spooked by as we have been by these acts, the spectral shows put on by whatever it is that haunts Hawk Mountain would have been more than enough spice for the evenings there.

Some incidents were comparatively simple, and perhaps rooted in natural, not *super*natural happenstance.

The drivers of the motorcoaches have tasted the flavor of the supernatural smorgasbord of Hawk Mountain on several occasions.

They were hard-pressed to explain the time when, after all the stories had been told, the haunted sites visited, and most fears subsided, the drivers went to warm-up their buses, only to find the batteries on both buses deader than doornails.

Another driver swears still today that it was a driverless car that hit the front bumper of his bus and then sped away along the road which leads past

Schambacher's grave. Damage to the bus was minimal. Damage to the bus driver's psyche was inestimable. On the whole, he'd rather have drawn an assignment to an Atlantic City casino that night!

More than one visitor has heard the faint, wispy sound of flute music filtering through the walls of the lower level of the old Schambacher place.

It is believed the crude music is the ghostly refrain of a young girl, who toots away eternally on a pennywhistle she clutched in a death grip when she fell down steps and broke her neck in that same dwelling many years ago.

The maiden was a deaf-mute, who never let go of the miniature flute in life, and, apparently in death. It is said she would play the little instrument to please her mother, while never herself hearing the sounds she made.

One day, as her parents were just outside the house, the little girl was scampering through the first floor when she fell through an open hatchway which led to the cellar. The fall was fatal.

Her parents, who spoke only German, returned to the house, only to find the broken body of their beloved daughter crumpled on the cellar floor.

Perhaps the muffled conversations often heard in the first-floor rooms of the house still today are those of the grief-stricken couple. Their traumatic experience may well have left an indelible, sometimes audible, mark inside the house. The talking heard by some in the house seems to be in German, and is centered in an area of the present living at which the floor-door to the basement was once located.

When that hatchway was removed, other alterations were made inside the building. These changes may have sealed the spirits inside.

Those who have lived in, visited, or researched the Schambacher house have had myriad experiences which would send the person of even the strongest constitution packing.

Light switches flicking up and down on their own; faucets turning themselves on and off; a bed vibrating and levitating; strange beams of light extending from floor to ceiling; the conversations, the sound of the pennywhistle; the muted sound of screams and the footsteps which seem to come out of nowhere and gradually fade.

Each encounter, no matter how nerve-shattering or subtle, seems designed to challenge those who dare to test the powers that hold Hawk Mountain in their grips.

On one Ghost Tour, approximately 80 participants witnessed a totally unexplainable glow in the cemetery which sprawls over the hillside beyond Schambacher's grave.

There was no doubt in anyone's mind (especially those who cowered in the buses in fear) that the glow was not a prank. It seemed to move unabated through the graveyard, just beyond the reach of those who took off after it.

Another band of visitors to the mountain experienced the gut-wrenching rumbling and ear-teasing squeals which have no earthly explanation.

Around the Schambacher house, there is a very good chance a stone wall to the rear will seem to take on a silvery glow; that a dim light will appear, fade, and re-appear in an upper-floor window; or that ghostly images will form in the side yard, in the vicinity of an old persimmon tree near where it is said Schambacher buried one or more of his victims.

Yes, this place is "magical," in a sense, and "menacing" in another. Whatever haunts the mountain is to be met with maturity, not mocked. It is to be feared, perhaps, but respected, for certain.

Psychics and mediums (and there have been many) who have investigated the spirits (and there are many) of the mountain declare the high hill to be among the most "haunted" places in all of America. The energy there, they agree, is powerful and plentiful.

The pathetic little girl's ghost seems to dominate the interior of the old tavern, while spirits believed to be those of the murder victims are strongest just outside the building.

As for Matthias Schambacher, the evil killer, his ghost is, in the words of one medium, "all around the mountain."

There are other ghosts, and other ways in which they manifest themselves. A great white "ghost bird" has been spotted on the mountain, elusive and unidentifiable even by veteran birders who have seen it.

Hawk Mountain is not a hell-hole of horror. It is a lovely, peaceful place with a world-class bird sanctuary, breathtaking scenery, and friendly people. They live, work and play on the mountain, and tend it with loving care.

Still, there are times when the energy, the *ghosts* of Hawk Mountain make themselves very well known.

One trance-medium, who helped identify some of the ghosts on the mountain, concluded, "It's like an incident happened here and somehow began to whirl or began to grow. I feel there is a lot of energy and the energy is very good. But at the same time, inside of that energy, there are events that took place here which have not been balanced."

Jim Brett, the sanctuary curator and keeper of the legends of the mountain, is philosophical about the balance of natural and supernatural energies there.

"I've been on that mountain since 1948," he says. "You can just feel it. Something strong is overwhelming you.

"My grandfather was a powwow doctor and once he took us kids to a furnace where he worked. He said he'd show us the devil inside the furnace. He opened the door and damned if we didn't see a figure, crouched down, laughing at us! My grandfather slammed the door.

Lehigh Valley Ghost Stories

"Up here, I've seen that same thing," Brett confides, with an eyebrow on his weathered face arched over a steely eye. "I've seen it walking up the road at night. I've looked over, and I have seen it.

"Maybe it's just my imagination, but... ."

His words trail off. Sometimes he, and others who live and/or work on the mountain, would rather not talk, or even think about, some of what goes on up there.

•

Does the ghost of a Civil War soldier ride atop his horse near Palmerton?

An old story claims that a young woman whose husband had left her to fight, dreamed continuously of her wayward lover.

One night, she dreamed she was swept away by a ghostly form atop a white horse. It was her husband!

In the darkness, the soldier cried out, "Brightly shines the moon...swiftly ride the dead!"

The phantom steed carried the couple to a cemetery, where it deposited them at a freshly-dug grave.

She awoke the next morning, and soon was given the bad news: Her soldier husband had died in a battle!

Lehigh Valley Ghost Stories

THE RED STREET GHOST

Back in days of old, when the township road which links the crossroad villages of Stony Run (then Wessnersville) and Stine's Corner, was called "Die Rote Schtross" by those who spoke Pennsylvania German.

The "Red Street" they called it, because its dirt surface was reddish in color, due to the clay content of the soil in that western edge of Lynn Township, Lehigh County. It is still known to locals as "Red Road."

It is along this "Red Street" that the eternal spirit of old Jacob Rubright can be seen, if all conditions are right.

For generations, the man's ghost has been gliding alongside the road, spooking the unaware humans who come across him and sending dogs into barking and howling frenzies.

"Nau geht der alt Tcheeck Ruprecht widder die Rote Schtross naus," the old-timers used to say, assuring each other that when the hounds would howl and the livestock would shuffle uneasily in their stalls, old Jake Rubright's ghost was on the move.

88

Lehigh Valley Ghost Stories

Tradition has it that Jacob Rubright's wraith is in search of a dead neighbor it believes to be in the same vacuum of time and reality in which it dwells.

Jake passed from this earth sometime before the turn of the twentieth century. He was in his mid-sixties, and may have taken to his grave the solution for a legendary feud which played out between two headstrong neighbors.

The valley just to the south of The Red Street used to be called Camp's Valley (or, in the dialect, Kompa Dahl), because one man, Andreas Camp, owned much of the property in that valley. The valley is now commonly known as Kemp's Valley.

The rest of the land was owned by Will Zimmerman.

The boundary between the two farms was a black-oak tree whose branches spread over The Red Street.

There was one strip of land, only about a half acre, which Zimmerman and Camp held in dispute. The overlapping strip led to bitter court battles, and an enduring and sometimes violent family squabbles.

Local lore holds that the final decision was made by Lehigh County Court in 1907, and the land was deemed part of Zimmerman's farm.

There was one problem: Will Zimmerman was dead for many years, and his survivors had sold the farm.

Andreas Camp still lived on his farm, but the

decision in the court did not sit well with him.

After the new owners of the Zimmerman spread moved to claim the land which they were awarded, Camp allegedly fired a shotgun blast their way.

Chasing them away, Camp then had a fence erected between the properties, with the disputed strip on his side.

The new owners tore down the fence. Camp built a more substantial one. It, too, was torn down.

Camp persisted by placing heavy beams and crossboards on what he determined to be the dividing line.

The new owner was equally persistent, bringing his team of horses and a wagon to the new fence. He hooked up a rope to a fence post and urged the horses on.

So deeply-rooted was the post beam that the wagon was upset as the tugging steeds met an irresistible force. The owner of the old Zimmerman farm tumbled out, and the wagon rolled on top of him, crushing him to death.

While some say it is *this* man's ghost which haunts The Red Street, the more likely prospect would be Jacob Rubright.

Those who have met the specter describe him in detail: He is of medium height and build; late sixties or early seventies; a close-cropped, gray beard; a narrow, high forehead.

He is dressed in dark, brown pants, a collar-less

coat, and a wide-brimmed hat.

The ghost may appear as if out of nowhere, the headlights of a car catching him as unaware and surprised as the passing motorist.

A word of warning: The ghost of Jake Rubright speaks only Pennsylvania "Dutch." Those brave enough to strike up a conversation with the apparition will be confronted with a a declaration and a question.

"Ich bin der Tscheeck Ruprecht un ich wuhn doh hiwwe im Eiledaal," he will say. Translated, it is "I am Jacob Rubright, and I live over in Owl Valley."

He will ask directions, or perhaps for a ride, to Willie Zimmerman's farmhouse.

Those who know the story will tell him Zimmerman has been dead for many years. He will deny that. "Ei, ich hab ihn yuscht vergeschter gsehne," he will insist, meaning he has seen him the day before yesterday.

He will seem confounded by the situation, and repeat, "Ich muss ebbes recht mache," which means "I must make something right."

With that, the ghost of Jacob Rubright will vanish into the night air, to resume its endless quest.

Nobody knows how many times this eerie scenario has played out.

Just what information Jake Rubright may have had, and whatever he could have "made right" will never be answered.

Perhaps, in life, he could have resolved the

Zimmerman-Camp land dispute. Perhaps, in life, he could have prevented the latter-day land owner's death.

We, and he, shall never know.

What we do know is that the ghost of the old man from Owl Valley is doomed to forever wander along the lonely road they used to call The Red Street.

•

Our granddaughter was killed in an automobile accident four years ago at the age of 20.

My husband had a total hip replacement and when he returned home, he was lying in his hospital bed. I was sitting on a recliner next to him.

All of a sudden, the wind chime hanging on the wall above us rang. Just once.

Now, this wind chime had never rung since I hung it up about 15 years ago.

There is absolutely no breeze where it hangs. My husband is not a believer in things of this nature, but we just looked at each other.

Could it have been our granddaughter dropping in to check on her pappy?

We would like to think so!

...Marie Moyer, Alburtis

Lehigh Valley Ghost Stories

THE GHOST, uh,
THE *GUEST* ROOM

The former parsonage of the First Presbyterian Church in Easton is the locale for this time-told tale of haunting.

The story has been handed down through many of the leading families of early Easton, and is attributed originally to Dr. Joseph Swift, who with his wife, Betsy, lived in a house which faced Center Square.

Elisha Allis, an 1885 graduate of Lafayette College and collector of city legends, recorded the tale, and it eventually found its way into the annals of the Northampton County Historical Society.

They called it, simply, "Easton's Ghost," and those who have professed knowledge of it "had seen a strange, vanishing figure so often that they thought nothing of it."

The figure appeared, and disappeared, inside and outside what was the parsonage of the First Presbyterian Church, later Churchman's Business College.

"Among accounts of the apparition was that of

the Nightingale family," related Mrs. William Hay in a presentation to the Fortnightly Club in Easton in 1948. "They told of a strange woman on the doorstep. When questioned, she suddenly vanished."

Mrs. Hay, who once lived in the building, says all who had any connection with it either heard the story, or had a personal contact with the spirit.

"One of the pastors in our day was Mr. Crane, who was told soon after his arrival that the house in which he was living had a ghost," she recalled. "I, too, was told it was haunted."

A former resident recalled an interesting encounter with the ghost. "I slept in the ghost room, and the ghost never bothered me," she said.

In time, the afflicted room became a guest room, and, on the occasion that two Methodist ministers were staying there for a week, the ghost made itself quite evident.

"Father was in his study, which commands a view of the doorway of this room. Looking up, he saw a figure disappearing into this room. He went right over to see if he could do anything for his guest, and found the room perfectly empty. He was so certain he had seen someone that he looked in the closet and in the bathroom, but found no one.

"We laughed over it, talked about our 'ghost' for a while, and then forgot it. Until, that is, a friend came to visit us.

"In the morning, mother said to her, 'I hope you

slept well.' She answered, 'No, I didn't.' Then, she said, 'I think you have a ghost in that room!'

"She said she was awakened by a noise, which did not last long. She said it sounded like mice or rats. Then, she was almost asleep when she felt a hand on her head. Thinking she had been dreaming, she tried to go off again, but was restless all night."

This kind of episode was repeated often in that room, with at least one visitor reporting they actually saw the shadowy figure they could best describe as a ghost.

•

SWEET MAGNOLIA EVANS

A tale of young, unrequited love forms the basis of the story of the haunting of the elegant Magnolia's Vineyard, in Guthsville.

The old building has a colorful history. Built in 1850, it was the centerpiece of the South Whitehall Township, Lehigh County, village.

Replacing a log house which stood on the site, the structure housed a post office and was a way-station along the stagecoach line.

In more recent years, it was the Guthsville Playhouse, in which many stars of stage and screen brought joy to audiences.

At the time of this writing, it is Magnolia's Vineyard, and its chef and owners bring joy to the palates of those who visit their fine-dining, Victorian dining room.

Before its warming hearth proves to be an apt setting to ponder the sad "Sonnet of Magnolia Evans" which graces the menu.

> *Fair of face and filled with fancy,*
> *a blossom of a girl,*

Lehigh Valley Ghost Stories

Magnolia's face was porcelain ivory,
framed with sable curls.

For the building's owners and restaurateurs, Caryn and Mark Rogosky, it was love at first site. They had been scouting the region for a place to house their concept of a restaurant, and placed a deposit on the old hotel a week after they first laid eyes on it.

And then, they found the diary.

Inside a 19th century family Bible was the diary of Magnolia Evans. The name rolled from their lips, and onto the sign for their new, as yet unnamed restaurant.

The daughter of a Major-General
(the Union Army's best)
He named Magnolia for the flower
that bloomed beyond the crest.

The girl's name, the setting along the Jordan Creek, and the look of the building, were almost too convenient. A legend, and a very romantic legend at that, was born.

As Magnolia walked, one dewy morning
along the vineyard road,
A handsome, black-eyed, mustached stranger
stopped her as she strode.

The story is a classic. As the sonnet goes, Magnolia Evans encountered the stranger, only to become embroiled in what would become a heartbreaking tale of lust, love, and supreme irony.

His rugged face was strong and silent,
His boots were packed with clay,
With a gasp, Magnolia noticed,
his uniform was gray!

Suffice to say, Magnolia (the daughter of "the

Union army's best Major-General") was caught off guard.

The rebel soldier seemed to accost poor Magnolia, as he pulled her into the orchard next to the Jordan Creek.

It was then that Magnolia noticed he had been wounded. Blood splattered his clothing. He was growing weak. He was winning Magnolia's heart.

She did all she could to soothe his pain.

For fifteen days Magnolia nursed him
until his strength regained,
And on the sixteenth night he loved her,
and she begged him to remain.

Of course, he could not tarry. She knew as well as he that to stay would be dangerous. The morning after their amorous encounter, he bid her farewell.

His tears were brimming and as he kissed her
he swore upon his life,
That when that blasted war was over
he'd take her for his wife.

They made a solemn pledge to meet after the Civil War, and agreed that the rendezvous spot would be in that orchard by the Jordan Creek.

The Confederate soldier never returned. No one knows if he died in battle, or returned to a lover in the south.

Whichever, it mattered not to Magnolia Evans. Dutifully, with her heart breaking into more pieces as the days turned to weeks, the weeks to months, and the months to years, she kept a vigil for her lost love.

Hers was a sad story, as witnessed in the final

lines of the sonnet.

One hundred years have passed since then,
but I've often heard it told,
You still can hear Magnolia weeping,
along the Vineyard Road.

And perhaps, just perhaps, you can hear Magnolia Evans weeping when you visit the restaurant which now occupies the site of sweet Magnolia's home.

As the flames flicker and cast warm shadows in the dining room, be on the lookout for the spirit of Magnolia Evans, which is supposedly still in and around the old hotel.

Several waitresses and diners claim to have felt the presence. There have even been sightings what appears to be a disconsolate young maiden in the foyer, dining rooms and kitchen.

Residents nearby say they've heard the story, and have come across a mysterious young woman from time to time, actually waiting down by the Jordan, staring blankly into space. As they try to identify or contact the figure, it fades into a transparent form and eventually disappears.

It is said that every night thereafter,
Magnolia would return,
To wait beside the flowing Jordan
for her lover, she would yearn.

•

A JOHNSONVILLE POLTERGEIST

Try these on for size: The sound of chains rattling in the next room; items moving by themselves on tables and a fireplace mantel.

It is the stuff of a rather unsettling experience.

For the residents of a property along Totts Gap Road in Johnsonville, it was almost *de rigeur*.

In a large, yellow house there, Martin Barsnica and his family had their share of unexplainable incidents.

"A couple time we heard what we though were kids coming down the stairs," he said. "We looked, and there was nobody.

"A couple times, we thought we heard chain. A few times, there was stuff moved off the fireplace mantel. It was too high for the kids to reach, and I know neither my wife nor I moved them."

Barsnica said there was proof positive that the items had moved. "You could tell where they were sitting originally from where the dust marks were."

Strange things continued to happen in the house. And, they began to take their toll on the family.

"Once, my youngest boy came downstairs and started beating on his older brother. He yelled that if he ever stood over him, on top of his bed again, he'd punch him. Thing is, it wasn't the oldest boy standing over him.

Another time, in fact quite frequently, when my wife would go down to the basement to do the wash, she'd get locked in. I mean, there was no way for the latch to spin over and actually hook up!"

The old house was once owned by an undertaker, but was not used for funeral purposes. It was also once a smokehouse, and it *was* used as a slaughterhouse. If nothing else, these facts add to the, er, *flavor* of the old place.

Tucked in the extreme northeastern corner of Northampton County, in Upper Mt. Bethel Township, the house on Totts Gap Road has continued to tease its present owners.

Carol Mucklin's experiences are chilling.

"I was going to bed quite early a couple times, and when I did, I noticed there was something standing at the bottom of my bed every time I would lay down.

"All of a sudden, I'd feel like something was at the bottom of my bed, or I'd feel someone was in the room with me," she said.

The situation grew so fearful that she kept a flashlight right over her head, on the headboard of the bed.

Carol believes the ghost is that of a young boy

who once resided in the house. She reckons he crossed to the other side at about age ten or eleven.

The eerie sensation that someone was in the room with her swept Carol on many occasions over about a two week period. More and more, she would be able to make out the form of a young boy.

"Finally," she said, "I got to the point I was really worried about seeing this.

"I looked down at the end of the bed and I said, 'It is fine that you're standing there. You can go away now. I'm not worried about what you're going to do!' After that, I never saw it again."

What she did see was the fairly clear outline of a young boy. She could not discern any facial features.

Brian Mucklin, Carol's teenage son, has also been touched, literally, by whomever, or whatever, it is that has provided goosebumps for those who have lived in the house.

Once, when he had fallen asleep while watching a late movie, Brian was awakened by the touch of a disembodied hand on his shoulder.

He said he positively felt it, quickly looked around to see who it was, but found nothing.

Carol Mucklin also reported items moving on countertops, and other untoward occurrences in the house.

The building is more than 125 years old, and many modifications and improvements have been made to it over the years.

This fact may contribute to the possibility that a level of spirit energy has been released, as detailed in the introduction to this book.

Whatever, Carol never feared for herself, or her children. The ghost was never threatening, and seemed more pathetic than psychotic.

After all, when she demanded it leave, it did.

Or did it?

Only time will tell.

•

INSTITUTES OF HIGHER HAUNTINGS

The Lehigh Valley is blessed with many fine colleges and universities.

In turn, many of those fine colleges and universities are cursed with many fine ghost stories.

From Kutztown to Lafayette, the places of higher learning throughout the valley have their legends, and their lairs in which spirits are said to taunt all who pass by.

By their very nature, these schools and those who populate them on both the student and faculty sides are diverse in their acceptance of, and open-mindedness toward the possibility that phantoms walk the corridors and rooms of their refined institutions.

Certainly one of the most charming colleges in the area, and in the country, is Moravian, in Bethlehem.

Again, because of its affiliations, the talk of ghosts there tends to ruffle some feathers. Still, those who are willing to discuss the notion are very convincing that the classically handsome buildings harbor things that go bump in the night.

The rumors and legends abound. Tales which

tell of a vast network of underground tunnels beneath the streets of Bethlehem have found their way into Moravian's South Campus.

The reports of unearthly subterranean sounds in some buildings is the product of the supposition that mysterious catacombs lace the land beneath them.

Another story concerns Main Hall, a women's dormitory on the South Campus.

There is a recurring legend there of an enchanted mirror in which the images of an elderly couple can be seen from a vantage point on a certain sofa.

If a young, unmarried couple, seated on that sofa, witnesses this phenomenon, they will eventually marry.

Students claim to still see the ghost of a Revolutionary War-era nurse which glides through the secluded practice rooms of the music department in the Single Brethren's House, one of the oldest (1748) buildings on campus. It originally housed the single men of the original Moravian community in Bethlehem.

That building, in which George Washington was hosted in 1783, also served as a hospital on two occasions during the Revolution.

On the grounds of the Main Campus is Comenius Hall, the central classroom and faculty office building on of Moravian.

Within its walls is the imprisoned spirit of a young man, said to have met his fate sometime around

World War I.

Nearby on Main Street on the north side of town is the Phi Mu Epsilon sorority house, and in it is the ghost of a poor girl remembered only as "Alicia."

Pledges are told that Alicia was killed on the attic steps when her boyfriend shoved her during an argument.

Those who have stayed in one of the two rooms in the attic say the faint outline of a phantom woman has been seen on several occasions.

A story with some similarities comes out of Kutztown University, where a dead coed is said to stroll the halls of the 1893-era Old Main.

And, said not to.

Nobody's really sure when the restless, hapless spirit of "Mary" was first spotted in the landmark campus building.

Every generation of students in recent decades has had its share of those who swear they've seen, felt, or heard the ghost.

Where Mary supposedly lived and died has been off limits to students for many years. Most recently, that fifth floor has served as an equipment storage area.

Her spectral impact has spread throughout the building, apparently.

What's more, while Mary's presence sends chills through the mortal souls of students in Old Main, Mary herself may have a companion.

That's the opinion of Lorraine Warren, who with her husband, Ed, make up a renowned team of psychic researchers and self-proclaimed "ghost busters" out of Milford, Connecticut.

In a 1991 visit to Kutztown University, the Warrens determined that the notorious fifth floor is indeed inhabited by the ghost of a young woman, likely in her twenties. She is doomed to spend an eternity there, they claimed, because of some sort of guilt.

A second presence, that of an older woman, can be felt in a small room near the elevator doors of the fifth floor.

That younger spirit is, apparently, Mary. It is said she committed suicide in Old Main shortly after discovering that she was pregnant. Just how she killed herself is a matter of debate.

Since her death, presumably around the turn of the century, students have reported odd happenings in the big building.

Some are relatively simple: Rapid temperature changes, disembodied footsteps, dining utensils gliding across tables.

Some are more complex.

"I have actually seen the ghost," proclaimed Beth, a student from Philadelphia who lived in Old Main. "She was, well, sort of homely, and she had dusty blonde hair and was wearing a light blue robe. You may think I'm crazy--hell, I thought I was crazy--but I know what I saw."

Beth, who preferred we not use her last name, was adamant. "I saw this, this *person* or whatever, first, and then I heard the stories. Funny thing, too, I saw her standing by the elevator door.

"I must tell you, I am into ghosts, and am a true believer. It is not the first time I saw something from the other side. Down home, I have often seen the ghost of an old man who used to live in my aunt's house. But please, don't think I'm some sort of weirdo. I put it all in perspective."

Beth heard about Mary after she told someone about her sighting. She heard Mary killed herself by hanging herself in Old Main, and heard that she became pregnant after having a one-night fling with a janitor.

"She seemed shy and withdrawing, and seemed to cower as I looked at her," Beth continued. "It was actually a rather pitiful sight, and not at all frightening."

Another version of the story includes a ghostly dog, said to have been with Mary when she killed herself. The howling of the dead dog can still be heard echoing through the long hallways of Old Main, they say.

Some incidents in Old Main dorm rooms really do defy any rational explanation. Take, for example, the time a student accidentally spilled water on her clock radio. She unplugged the radio and set it aside to dry. Moments later, the unplugged, non-battery backup radio started playing, loud and clear.

Or, consider the water that flows freely from unturned faucets; the mournful moaning sounds that seem to billow from the elevator shaft; or countless other incidents which catch the students of Old Main off guard on a regular basis.

Because the legend is so powerful and the alleged experiences so numerous, the university administration has taken note, and has done its best to downplay any thoughts of a haunting at Old Main.

The week before Halloween, 1991, William A. Yurvati, a library technician in the archives of the Rohrbach Library at K.U., presented a paper in which he hoped the ghost of Old Main would be put to rest.

His diligent work did tidy up some of the rough edges of the "Mary" story.

One version is that the girl hanged herself in, or threw herself down the elevator shaft in the late 1800s. Yurvati pointed out it would had to have been very late in the 1800s since the elevator was not installed until the 1899-1900 school year.

In addition to the pregnancy theory, it has been repeated that Mary's ghost haunts Old Main because she died in the building the day before she was to graduate. She remains earthbound, and Old Main-bound, in search of a diploma she was denied by death.

Poring through the records of what was then the Keystone State Normal School, Yurvati came across a find which could have been the very genesis of the "Mary" tales.

There *was* a Mary. Of course, there have been

many Marys over the decades at K.U. But *this* Mary, this Mary S. Snyder, could well have been *the* Mary who had a reason to remain in Old Main.

In Mary Snyder's story, there is no janitor, no noose, no elevator shaft, no pregnancy, no suicide.

Mary, age 22, was a farmer's daughter from Limekiln, Berks County, was one of the 100 members of the class of 1895. She had completed her studies in college, had successfully finished her final exams, and was looking forward to graduation day on June 27, 1895.

Shortly after completing her finals, Mary complained of pain. She retired to rest and prepare for her graduation.

In the middle of the night before what would have been a glorious day for Mary, she died. The cause of death was congestive heart failure, brought on by inflammatory rheumatism. The normal school commencement exercises went on as planned, with the class members marching through town in an early morning rain and into the college chapel for the graduation program.

There was a pall over the ceremony, however, as class members had learned of Mary Snyder's death the day before.

Black crepe badges were made, and each member of the class wore one in mourning. They pledged to keep wearing them for 30 days.

"Her life as a student brought out a noble

character," a notice in the *Normal Vidette* school newspaper said of Mary. "She was possessed of more than ordinary intelligence and made very good use of her time."

More poignantly, the article concluded, "She showed by her life that while she conscientiously attended to all her duties as a student, she did not live alone for this life. While we sadly mourn her departure, we yet have the blessed assurance that death to her meant eternal bliss."

In his writings, Yurvati stopped short of totally denying the ghost stories of Old Main.

"The true story of Mary's death appears to be the origin of the legend concerning ghostly happenings in Old Main," he said. "Although these facts do not support or debunk the proclaimed sightings of the Old Main ghost, they offer an explanation behind a legend that has persisted for many years.

"Perhaps the memory of her untimely death, perpetuated by the legend of Mary, the ghost of Old Main, serves to remind us of our own mortality and the value of living each day to the fullest."

There are at least two ghosts on the campus of Muhlenberg College. One is in the Bernheim House, and is affectionately called "Oscar" by those who have felt its presence.

"Oscar" is Oscar Bernheim, who donated the building to the college. The former college registrar, commons manager and alumni secretary died in a third floor bedroom in the house, and some say his spirit never left.

There is an unusual twist to the story of Oscar's ghost. The story has been handed down that when he donated the house to the college, he was assured that his beloved rose garden would be maintained in perpetuity.

Sometime along the way, after Oscar's death, that agreement was forgotten. Another gentleman, who had been an enemy of Oscar's donated money for the erection of a residence hall. That gent stipulated it be built on what was Oscar's precious garden.

Oscar's ghost returned to haunt the place.

The stories involve incidents in the basement, attic, and the room in which Oscar died. Women who have lived in the house say they have felt his presence, and some claim to have seen the wispy image of a diminutive man. When shown a photograph of Oscar Bernheim, they invariably say, "That's him! That's the face I saw!"

At Cedar Crest College, it is "Wanda" who is the resident ghost of Butz Hall since her death by her own hands in 1956.

While that's the prevailing story at the Allentown west side campus, there is nothing in the school records that indicates a girl named Wanda, or in fact any girl, died there in 1956.

Still, Wanda's ghost is the culprit when anything unusual happens at Butz.

Lehigh Valley Ghost Stories

In a 1991 interview in *Lehigh Valley Life* magazine, W. Ross Yates, professor emeritus of government at Lehigh University and a valley historian of note, flatly denied the existence of any ghosts at Lehigh U.

"Lehigh University is devoid of ghosts," he stated, unequivocally. "It is a school devoted to science, and therefore it has no room for ghost stories. There are no dead janitors lurking in the halls."

All well and good, Prof. Yates. But what about the pesky ghost which has pestered patrons and professionals alike in the Linderman Library?

Indeed, the folks at Lehigh are tight-lipped about their resident ghost, but stories continue to circulate regarding the somewhat bedraggled old cuss. One library employee said, "was a pain in the butt when he came here in life, and is a bigger pain in the butt now, when he comes back as a ghost."

•

Is the Pennsylvania House apartment building in Walnutport haunted? Resident Reynold Mummey thinks it might be.

Mummey says, "I've been in bed at night looking in the hallway, and there will be a black shadow which can't be cast from any window because there's no windows in there. I'd hear noises sometimes, and sometimes music that sounds like ballroom dance music." He says others who have spent time there have seen and heard it, too.

A REGAL WRAITH

The King George Inn has been a landmark on the Easton-to-Reading Road (now Route 222), since the French and Indian War.

After the hostilities with the natives subsided, the field behind old Dorney's Tavern was the site of militia and army drilling and training.

Many a weary man and woman alighting from a passing wagon dusted off the road dirt and entered the portals of the way station on the busy crossroads.

Folks who were settling the growing area gathered there to discuss politics, religion, and the travails of 18th, 19th and now 20th century life.

It is a *very* historic site. So historic, in fact, that it in America's Bicentennial year of 1976, the National Park Service designated it as a National Historic Site.

It is also a very *haunted* historic site.

Duffy Schiffner is the no-nonsense kind of guy, affable but unflappable, you'd expect to have seen for more than a dozen years behind the bar of the elegant King George Restaurant.

He, his fellow employees, and especially Cliff

114

Lehigh Valley Ghost Stories

McDermott, the owner of the fashionable eatery, know well the proud tradition of the tavern, hotel and dining rooms. They also know of the ghosts which walk in their midst.

Duffy recalled the time he was upstairs in the office, alone.

"I heard a noise," he says, "and I hollered. I thought it was a cab driver, maybe. Nothing. Then, I heard the noise again, and I called out again. Nothing. Then, there was this sharp drop in the temperature. I mean it got freezing, all of a sudden and just in that one place. Then, I heard this strange sort of tinkling sound. I know I was alone, and I'll never figure all that out!"

McDermott, a New York native whose Irish pride shows in the decor of the downstairs tavern and the Inn's legendary St. Patrick's Day parties, has owned the place since 1970, and has heard practically all the old stories about it.

Sometimes, though, the stories come not from within, but from without.

McDermott was relaxing in the downstairs bar as he agreed to re-tell some of the stories. Fittingly, as the conversation turned from introductions to Ireland and things Irish, to the supernatural, he sauntered toward the stereo to turn down the haunting strains of the overture from "Phantom of the Opera."

The stage was set.

"We had a psychic here one Saturday evening," McDermott recalled. "I expected to see somebody like, well, you know, what you'd think of as a *psychic*. Instead, it was this nice-looking blonde, about 35 or so. We were really busy, and I didn't have much chance to talk to her, but she said she saw someone standing in the hallway with a child!"

Cliff shook his head and arched his eyebrows as he continued. "She saw a woman with a small child. Both were in period dress, you know, eighteenth century. She said she definitely saw a silhouette of them, up there in the entranceway.

"Then, she came down here, and she went in this room here (pointing to the front dining room), and said, 'you know, I think there's money in this wall somewhere.'"

At that, McDermott chuckled. He said he did not discount the woman's claim, but kidded that, "if that's the case, where's my sledgehammer?!"

"That's all true, though," he added. "She said there were the presences of a mother and child, and gold coins inside a wall."

McDermott then related other stories he's heard about the building, some of which may relate to experiences people have had in the inn.

"There are a couple of hand-me-down stories about the place," he said. "The downstairs used to be only accessible from a staircase in the back corner. It was an all-dirt floor then, and it had this gigantic furnace right in the middle. It was a converted coal furnace. You had to bend down to walk down here, and it was a very scary place.

"During World War II, supposedly, a woman working in the scullery, washing dishes by hand upstairs, came down to hang linens to dry. She turned the lights out for some reason, and was frozen with fear, literally."

The woman wound up cowering in the darkness, under the spell of an unseen force and fear. After a couple hours, crew people upstairs finally discovered her in what was then the dank basement, hysterical.

"She told them she had heard the sound of a baby, crying, coming from the cistern," said McDermott.

That cistern, or old well, was and is situated near the middle of the front wall of the downstairs room. It has since been, as has been the entire downstairs, cleaned up and restored and handsomely decorated.

Cliff McDermott continued the story. "Nobody thought anything of it until someone remembered that in 1756, during the local Indian uprisings, Indians used to attack places like the one which stood here. They'd swoop down and sometimes disembowel babies, and throw them down the wells to poison the water supply. There is a tale around here that a baby was really taken out on this site and met that fate."

That unfortunate woman, in that dark cellar that day, was not the only person to claim to hear the sound of a crying baby coming from that front wall.

It could well be that the anguished ghost of an innocent infant is another of the spirits of the King George. Cliff McDermott does not dismiss that possibility.

"When we first took over, I did have an experience. In the kitchen, I thought I heard that baby crying. Others have, too."

There may be more ghosts in the place.

Several years ago, a bus boy who McDermott described as very straight, sane, sober and sensible (he bussed there between terms at M.I.T.), went into a provisions room upstairs and told Cliff he felt the presence of someone else up there with him.

"He said he saw a man with a bright, red tunic, lace on the sleeves, and the man had a beard. This faint figure, he said, then threw it's head back as if it was laughing. But, the boy said, there was no sound.

"I know it sounds very Dickensian, but he was a trustworthy kid. I had no reason not to believe him."

Another story involves a man who supposedly hanged himself in a staircase which leads from the main floor upstairs. There is a possibility his ghost inhabits that area.

"One dark and stormy night," Cliff said, asserting that it really *was* a very *dark and stormy night,* "my brother and I were at the bar. He went up to the office, and came past the attic door. The door was open, and he closed it. We both knew it was latched. I just shrugged. Then, when I had to go upstairs, that door was open again. He went back up, and the same thing happened. We thought we were doing it to each other, but we weren't."

His proclivity for things ghostly may have been fine-tuned early in life. "The Irish," he noted, "for some reason or another, seem to have a sensitivity to this sort of thing. I never had any psychic powers, I don't believe, but my mother used to tell us stories about our old house in Staten Island, and how it was haunted. It used to give me the chills."

Cliff McDermott takes the ghosts of the King George in stride.

McDermott has a strong sense of time, place and history. He knows the human dramas which have played out inside the old building have not all be pleasant, but knows, too, that the energy inside the inn is harmless.

"Whatever we have here is not threatening. I'm in here alone a lot, and I think about all the things that must have happened here, and it's mind-boggling."

•

THE PHANTOM
IN THE BLACK TOP HAT

The setting is the far northeastern corner of Northampton County, beyond Bangor, along Ridge Road.

It was along that road, between Bangor and Johnsonville, that Mike Russo and his grandfather were driving one day in the late 1960s.

As they passed an old farmhouse, they unwittingly saw what they, and others, now call the "Ghost of Ridge Road."

"He was dressed in high-buttoned shoes, spats, and a black top hat," said Joe Russo. "He had his cane, and was sitting there, waving at us. My brother Mikey and my grandpop got so scared. Mikey said it was the ghost of Ridge Road, hit the road!"

The story goes that a man hanged himself sometime around the turn of the century in a large barn which once stood on the property they were passing.

Elmer Lohman, one of the keepers of the folk tale fires in the Five Points area, said a man really did hang himself there. Elmer, known to his friends as "Do

Me," said the suicide victim was an eccentric, middle-age man who was having domestic problems. He said the body wasn't discovered for several weeks after his deed.

Generations of folks up that way claim to have seen unusual sights and people there. Sometimes, the phantom would manifest itself as a long-haired woman. Sometimes, it was the man in the spats and top hat.

"All I know is that my grandpop and Mikey shook for two weeks," said Joe Russo. "Everytime they'd go past the place, grandpop would gun it."

That old farm has since been demolished, and new homes have been built on the site. But, the memories of its supernatural history still send shudders down the spines of many people.

Betty Goble now lives in Cape May Court House, N.J., but those memories linger, since she and her husband lived in the old farmhouse for 15 years.

"I'll tell you about what happened to me, but you'll laugh," she said.

"Try us," we said.

"Let me see, the first experience was when my mixer just shot up out of the bowl and across the room. And then, there's the time we had musical beer mugs on a shelf. In the middle of the night, one night, they all started playing. They were the kind, you know, you had to pick up before they would play."

And then, said Mrs. Goble, there was the time a friend of her sons was in from North Jersey, and was

121

touched by the spirit.

"The boy got so afraid he called his mother to come and get him the next morning," she remembered.

"Then, I had my nephews there. They were sleeping upstairs and I had an organ downstairs, and it started playing. Of course, that frightened them, but they thought it was really cool, and couldn't wait until the next night to see or hear what would happen!"

Eventually, the children took to holding amateur seances to try to conjure up the spirit. They claimed to have felt the presence on occasion. Betty's daughter, Alexis, said she was even kicked or shoved more than once by an unseen force.

One element in Betty's recollections follows suit with the concept of the "recording" of spirit messages on parts of a building, or the furniture within it.

"We had taken a floor heating vent grate out, and made a coffee table out of it. It seemed that the table had a lot to do with the ghost. Apparently, he liked that grate."

Betty Goble feels it is a strong energy that dwelled within the old house in which she and her family lived for before it was torn down.

"When we tried to tear down the old house, we had a bulldozer come in. They tied a cable around it and could not pull the place down. But, it cut the house in half, and the house just stayed put. It never fell or anything. We finally had to get another dozer to come in, and push the place down."

Did the destruction of the house send the ghosts packing? Betty Goble thinks not.

After the house was torn town, things started happening across the street. "We had two heavy, steel front doors, which we'd lock at night. Then, we'd get cold. We'd get up, and the doors were wide open. My husband got tired of that, so he nailed the doors closed, and son-of-a-gun, they opened up that night again!"

Betty and her husband, Hampton, told some friends about the incidents, and when the laughter died down, they resigned themselves to the reality that they were experiences very real incidents that to the uninitiated would seem very unreal.

"In fact, we had told Ruth and Bob Saltern, our friends, about it all, and Bob smiled and said I was full of it. Just as he said that, a picture fell off the wall. The hook and wire were intact, but the thing just dropped as he said what he said."

Betty's friend, Ruth, confirmed the stories. "When that house was torn down, those freed spirits just moved across the street with them."

Ruth Saltern remembered the very solid steel doors that did, indeed, open on their own at night.

"And," Ruth recalled, "they had a small dog. They used to throw a ball for the dog to fetch, and before it would hit the sliding doors, it would stop, like there was something there to stop it. That's when they told my husband about their ghost, and he told Betty she was, well, full of it."

And that was when the picture fell from its hook.

"It was so astonishing," Ruth exclaimed.

Betty said that old grate may have played a major role in all the paranormal activity.

"My daughter moved to New York, and she took the table with her. She had different experiences there. She had her Christmas tree on it, and she had walked into the house and the tree was on the other side of the room.

"She had her cat locked in the bedroom because she didn't like him running through the house, so it wasn't the cat that did it. Whatever it is, well, I don't know."

Jim and Bev Depopulous now live on the site of the old home and barn.

Jim has heard the stories, and admits that he's had some strange happenings take place there. To be on the safe side, shortly after they purchased the property, Bev performed her own style exorcism by walking around and encouraging the spirits to leave them be.

It seems to have worked. Then again, the old heating grate coffee table didn't come with the house!

•

THE GHOST AT
WIDOW BROWN'S
AND THE GHOST AT
WIDOW BROWN'S

The title of this chapter is not incorrect. You are not seeing double.

This is the story, or more properly, *these are the stories*, about the ghosts at the two Widow Brown's restaurants in the Lehigh Valley.

Who does not know of the Widow Brown's in Wescosville and/or the Widow Brown's in Stockertown?

But, who *does* know of the ghosts, or at least the unexplained events, at both locations?

John Nyari and his father own the Widows, and John said he is not oblivious to the stories of "things that go bump in the night" at the two restaurants.

"Oh, I've heard lots of them," the personable restaurateur confirmed.

"Especially about Marvin, up in Stockertown. The girls up there swear Marvin still is there. There's a back stairway in the one dining room which is the original part of the building.

"Marvin hanged himself in the back stairwell, or at least that's the rumor. The only experience I had up there which I thought was strange was in room 'B' next to the bar.

"The stereo system worked in the whole restaurant, everywhere, except in Room B.

"There are about six speakers in the room, up in the ceiling. Nobody can touch them. There was never any music in that room. The girls would laugh and say the music bothered Marvin.

"Oh, they'll tell you lots of stories up there," he concluded.

And they certainly did.

Chris Holva, manager of the Widow Brown's in Stockertown, said there have been many sightings and sensations which have been credited to Marvin, their resident ghost.

"There was a sighting of a shadow," Holva recalled. "The secretary's brother and husband were working here, at the bar, and they say they saw a shadow coming down the stairs. They described it as a white shadow. They don't know where it went, and certainly couldn't account for it."

Waitress Connie Bath said the eeriest incident she can recall was when three waitresses, all working the same night, all reported mysterious splotches of blood on their uniforms.

"Nobody could determine where it came from,"

she said. "It was on our shoulders. Neither of us was cut, and we weren't working with raw meat or anything."

Bath remarked that the incident took place on Valentine's Day a few years back. She quipped that the traditional "Night of Love" was a "Night of Blood" for the waitresses.

"Maybe," she mused, "Marvin was in mourning that night for a lost love."

Ray Steinmetz, who worked at the Stockertown landmark, said it is generally regarded that "Marvin" was an innkeeper there during a time the old stagecoach stop was an inn of somewhat ill repute. The theory is Marvin had an affair with one of the house ladies and was spurned. One version of the story is that he killed her, and them himself, in the hotel.

Shannon Flutter has worked at Widow Brown's for nearly 15 years. "Many years ago," she stated, "I was at the basement door, ringing up checks on the calculator. I turned around and saw the door handle to the basement door turn.

"There was nobody downstairs, nobody coming down the steps. I froze. I was scared. The handle turned, but nobody was there at all.

"Another time, a hostess named Louise went up the stairs to the attic. She was going up to get some papers. There was no wind, no windows open, no breeze at all. As she approached the papers she needed, a gust of wind came out of nowhere and blew them toward her. They landed at her feet."

Flutter remembered times the energy made itself known in even more profound ways.

"The restaurant was closed one night, and the manager and cleaning lady were the only ones here. The cleaning lady said she saw an old man, in old clothing, sitting at the bar, drinking from a beer stein.

"She thought the manager had left him in. She approached the manager, and he told her he didn't leave anyone in.

"The doors were locked, and nobody could have gotten in. When the cleaning lady was done talking to the manager, she returned to the bar, and the old guy was gone. The doors were still locked up tight."

At the Stockertown Widow Brown's, lights have turned themselves on and off, swinging doors have swung when they should not have, and on one occasion, a photograph taken of a customer revealed the distinct silhouette of an unseen person near the subject.

The Widow Brown's in Wescosville, once the Wescosville Hotel, also seems to have some ethereal energy pent up inside it.

A barmaid who chose to be identified only as Suzy, said whatever or whoever cohabits the old building is benign, and more felt than seen.

"Near the front of the restaurant area, you can walk there and feel something kind of make your hair rise," said Suzy, who added that it is a fairly common occurrence when lights go on and off with no human aid.

"I've had experiences here," she claimed. "I have walked through that area and have felt a definite cold pocket. It isn't where the vents are. There is no air coming in anywhere. It has happened to me, and at least one other waitress a few years ago."

Another waitress at the Wescosville Widow Brown's agreed that there is a strange sensation which seems to grip the front dining room of the restaurant.

"It's nothing bad," she said. "In fact, I really feel we have a kind and somewhat sad ghost here. As for Marvin, up in Stockertown, well, he's *their* problem!"

•

Some folks who have worked in the third floor meeting rooms of the Hotel Bethlehem report inexplicable incidents, sounds and sights in the rooms, behind the bar, and in the corridors on that floor.

The popular explanation is that a guest died (of natural causes) in one of the rooms to the rear of the bar, and his spirit continues to dwell within the walls of the historic and beautiful mid-city hotel.

...Anonymous Hotel Bethlehem employee

BURIED ALIVE!

f ar from the hustle and bustle of the Allentown-Bethlehem-Easton metropolitan area, in the very northern peak of Northampton County, is the Slateford Bridge.

Built to support now-defunct railroad tracks, the bridge has quite a history...and quite a ghost.

Warren Moore, who was 83 at the time of our interview with him, was a storehouse of lore about the span.

The Portland man said the bridge was built with concrete taken from the site of the present electric power plant. At the time, the land was mostly marsh.

During World War II, he recalled, there was a U.S. Army installation there, set up to protect the area against any possible sabotage. Moore says there are still pockmarks on the bridge, evidence of the times soldiers took idle shots at it.

Moore also said the bridge was built using cheap labor from men brought in from the Bowery section of Manhattan.

One of those men never made it out of the job

site alive.

Neal Brodt, a collector of regional photographs and folk tales, backed up Moore's recollections that an unfortunate laborer was indeed buried alive in concrete during the bridge construction in 1911.

The black man was in a concrete pouring crew when he slipped from his position and fell into the fresh cement. The pouring could not be halted, and the man was encased in the bridge piling.

To this day, his ghost can be felt and heard around, and *in*, the old bridge.

Michael and Chris Murray agree that their experiences in and near the old bridge have yielded their share of intimidation.

"It's very scary there," says Chris. "I'd never go there at night. But people actually camp out there! Not me!"

Michael Murray does not count the old bridge among his favorite places, either.

Once, he was walking home from work over the grafitti-scarred bridge. "I started to walk on top of it, and before I got on it, I heard a noise. I didn't know what it was, but it made me nervous. I froze for a minute and lit a match. I couldn't see anything because there was no moon.

"I got on the bridge, and just kept walking. I had this very eerie feeling something was behind me."

Maybe there was, Michael. Maybe there was.

•

A LYNCHED INDIAN'S REVENGE?

We first visited the handsome, haunted Maple Grove Hotel, near Alburtis, in the second volume of our *Ghost Stories of Berks County* trilogy.

The old country inn, once a stagecoach stop and hotel in the rich mill and mine country of the East Penn Valley, has undergone several changes since our first investigation there, not the least the changing of name to the Inn at Maple Grove.

One thing has not changed at the inn. It is haunted by a ghost they call Charlie.

The hotel was built by John Keifer in about 1783. Keifer had also built several grist and saw mills in the area, as well as homes for the mill workers. The inn was established to house suppliers and provide a diversion for his employees.

Today, it serves both neighborhood faithfuls and a growing clientele from the Reading and Allentown areas. Its location, between the two metropolitan regions and near the Doe Mountain Ski Area, ensures a steady base of customers.

The place has many interesting legends

attached to it.

It is recorded that Thomas Alva Edison, on one of his far-flung sprees from his lab in Menlo Park, N.J., used the Maple Grove Hotel as a base of operations while he conducted experiments in the area.

For our purposes, however, two more unpleasant tales prime the poltergeistic pump which seems to work overtime at what is now a fine-dining restaurant with charming atmosphere and lovingly-prepared food.

There is fair evidence that long ago, a guest at the old hotel was murdered on the second floor. And, an Indian was hanged, or better put, lynched, in what is now the main dining room.

For the stories about the possible aftermath of these incidents, we turned to Colin Heffley, whose family took over operation of the inn in 1977.

Heffley said the omens came early. As he was remodeling the building in the winter of 1977, an elderly man strolled up from a nearby farmhouse.

"The place is hexed," he said, in a thick Pennsylvania "Dutch" accent. "There are schpuks (spooks) in there!"

Just what Colin wanted to hear!

And yet, the very real possibility that ghosts do walk the floorboards of the inn eventually played a role in the development of the inn's image.

Heffley developed a logo which depicted what he called a "gentlemanly" ghost breezing through a doorway. The history of the hotel, as well as the stories of the deaths there, were detailed on the back of the menu.

Colin cared not a whit about the ghostly gossip.

"Right from the start," he related, "strange things happened.

"My brother Malcolm and I were working inside the common room one day when one of the local men wandered in and asked if we'd seen the ghosts yet. We chuckled, listened to his stories and kept working. All of the ghost stories and the tales of murder and Indians and everything so long ago kind of added another dimension to the place. It was not your ordinary, boring, country hotel!"

Colin says, however, that the stories of those "long ago" episodes started to merge with the present rather quickly.

"Later that same night, the old guy came in and asked again if we'd seen any ghost. My brother and I were working with an electric saw. Everything was going along fine until the saw quit on us.

"At first, we thought the thing just gave out, or maybe there was a mechanical problem. But, we traced things back to the wall plug. There it was, pulled from the socket. There was a whole bunch of extension cord curled up underneath it.

"It wasn't like it was stretched out and pulled out by our tugging on it. It was plugged in very firmly when we started, but something, or somebody, pulled it out of the socket. But we were the only people, at least the only *living* people, in the place!"

Certainly, a mysteriously-pulled plug does not a ghost story make. The fact that the plug was *put back into the socket,* and then pulled out, and then put back in again, several times, may still be flimsy evidence.

Still, for those two men on that dark night in that lonely, empty building, in that remote village, it was the start of a chain of events that more baffled than frightened them.

With the knowledge that some folks had labeled the place "hexed" and other had suggested the existence of ghosts in the old hotel, Colin and Malcolm half-heartedly attributed the nuisances to a generic ghost they named "Charlie."

The Heffley family's more profound brushes with their shadowy housemate failed to heighten their fears. Rather, they made them curious as to what really may have happened in the building they were to call home and work. Colin was steadfast.

"We have a theory about all of this," he told a reporter from the Allentown Call who came to do a story about the hotel's food and, er, spirits.

"We think it's the ghost of the Indian who was buried beneath the fireplace. His spirit never went wherever Indian souls are supposed to go. Every time we build a fire, it disturbs his rest. But he's a friendly ghost, and we expect to stay."

The Indian ghost legend is the most romantic, in

its own bizarre way, of the three possibilities that exist for the presence of a spirit in the Inn at Maple Grove.

The story is presented that the Indian was engaged in an affair with a white girl from the village. The girl became pregnant, and the villagers found out that the native was the father.

They decided to punish the Indian for his socially-unacceptable act. A kangaroo court was held, and the Indian, of course, was found guilty of a trumped-up charge.

The story also has it that the young lady was a willing partner in the act, but this was not good enough for the villagers, who lynched the man in front of the fireplace in what is now the dining room of the inn.

It is said that the Indian vehemently proclaimed his innocence of whatever charge was leveled against him. As the noose was being tightened around his neck, he vowed to remain earthbound and prove his innocence.

This proclamation notwithstanding, the infuriated and incensed white men kicked a stool from beneath the Indian's feet and his body writhed in pain as his neck snapped and he choked to death.

One version of the story claims that the victim was hastily and unceremoniously buried in the dirt floor of the basement of the hotel.

While none of the unexplained occurrences at the hotel can be linked directly with the Indian, or anything Indianesque, the fireplace does play a prominent role.

There is a massive, iron crane in the twelve-feet wide hearth. This cooking crane once started to shake, all on its own.

The Heffleys noticed it rattling a bit, and the rattle became a violent heaving that seemed to shake the entire building. Not even tornado-force wind directly down the chimney, nor several human strongmen could have done what was being done.

Colin remembered the shaking of the crane well.

"I heard it and saw it plain as day," he said. "I was working in the room when it happened. It was a bit scary, and I couldn't for the life of me figure out what could have caused it.

"We Pennsylvania Dutch have a convenient little way of backing out of things we don't understand. We say, 'yah, yah,' and shake our heads like we really do understand and try to figure it out later. That's what I did. I said, 'yah, yah,' and ran the hell out of there!"

The crane incident occurred in the period during which the building was being remodeled. It was the same time of the unplugging of the electric saw. One night during this time frame, Colin and his brother witnessed the flickering, the dimming and the brightening of lights in the building.

They looked at one another, goosebumps growing. Then, from the basement, they heard what Colin described as the main electrical switch being through up and down, rapidly, on and off. It was as if ghostly fingers were trying to give them a sign...and perhaps a warning.

About a week after the Heffleys opened their pride and joy on St. Patrick's Day, 1977, the family moved in to the rooms upstairs, above the bar and dining room.

Colin remembered, "We went to bed about two, maybe two-thirty in the morning, and fell asleep. It was a long, hard day. I recall my wife waking me up and in a loud whisper saying, 'wake up, there's somebody in our bedroom!!' I woke up and looked around.

"The bedroom door we had closed securely was wide open and the room was icy cold. It wasn't like a cold because of lack of heat, you know. It was an eerie kind of chill. I looked out the open bedroom door and noticed that the hallway light was off. We kept it on at night, but it was off!

"After a few minutes of trying to figure out what was going on, the bedroom door just slammed shut. We just stayed in bed, squeezing each other's hands until the sun came up."

The next morning, Colin remembered getting dressed and heading to a nearby store to buy a Sunday paper. He returned to the hotel, locked the door behind him and headed upstairs to the living quarters.

All was quiet in the building as he started up the steps. He took a few steps up, and heard a few steps.

It was not the sound of *his* footsteps.

He paused. He continued up the steps, and

again heard footsteps following him.

He distinctly heard the footsteps climb the stairs, and stop at has bedroom door. He looked around, but saw nothing.

There were many occasions when he and others heard mysterious footfalls on the staircase and in the hallway. Doors creaked open and shut.

On quiet nights, after the customers had left and the building was all but empty, the plaintive sound of whistling could be heard near the fireplace. Nothing recognizable, just nondescript, haunting melodies from ghostly lips.

A hatchway to the basement was covered during the renovation process. A rug now conceals the hatch, long unused and non-functional.

One time, again after the hotel had closed for the night, Colin heard a rapping sound coming from somewhere in the building. He looked out the main entrance and saw no one. He listened more attentively as the knocking continued in a non-rhythmic cadence. He cocked his head and eventually placed the source of the knocking at the center of the floor, where the hatchway was located. A search of the basement turned up nothing.

There have been episodes witnessed by, and experienced by, groups of customers. Some write them off as simply unexplainable and interesting, and some shrink in fear.

Lights have dimmed often. A jukebox suddenly

began to play on its own. Drinks have fallen from tables, and patrons claimed to have been pushed out of their chairs. The latter phenomenon, you say, may not be unusual for a tavern. But Colin assured us it was not the product of the *other* kind of spirits!

"Ever since we opened up," Colin said, "thing happened that have been unbelievable. A very big and heavy chandelier once started to sway ever so gently. A few of us noticed it and we kept watching until it was moving back and forth rather quickly.

"One time, and I still can't comprehend this, a table full of people all claimed that a salt shaker rose up about four or five inches into the air, opened up and spilled salt into the lap of one of the patrons.

"We've had psychics come in here and identify one spirit, that of a young woman, who was weeping near the fireplace. She told us not to worry, no harm would come."

Colin claimed that one night, after the hotel was closed and he was upstairs doing some paperwork, his wife and he noticed a scratching noise coming from his desk. The couple looked at the desk and his pocket calculator was levitating. It was floating in mid-air, a few inches above the desk top.

The Allentown Call reporter hit the mark when she noted, "Relating the ghost stories here is like doing the Louvre on roller skates."

There are so many mind-boggling incidents: Radios blasting when the volume dial was turned up by unseen hands; the family cat going into a frenzy in the middle of the night; the neighbor who believes the place to be "hexed;" and on, and on.

One neighbor once adorned the restaurant with a ceramic ghost with "The Spirit of Maple Grove" emblazoned on its sheet. The gift stood proudly on top of the cigarette machine.

Oddly enough, it was that symbolic spook that played a role in the reporter's own brush with the supernatural.

She got her story and readied her camera equipment for some accompanying photos. All was well, except for the flash attachment. The batteries were dead, although she swore they should have been more than strong enough to carry out the assignment.

She returned to the hotel after going to the closest store for a pack of fresh batteries. The photo session went well until the pictures were developed.

Then, Colin said, she reported a strange addition to the photograph of the ceramic ghost. A hitherto unseen band of light, resembling a string of white pearls, showed up ever so lightly in the background of the picture.

Evidence that something strange has been going on at the hotel continues to mount.

One night, a family of diners paid their bill near the door, said goodbye, and left. They gently pulled the door closed behind them.

Minutes later, frantic rapping was heard from

outside the main door. Colin couldn't figure out why anyone would be beating on the door. The place was open, and the door was unlocked.

But he was wrong. Somehow, the door had locked when the last patron left. Two slip bolts were latched. The bolts had somehow, and almost inconceivably, slid over into place, and locked!

Some people have reported actually seeing a ghostly presence inside the hotel. One barmaid reported seeing a mysterious old man seated at the bar. She remembered only that he must have come in when she wasn't looking, and had taken his place at the end of the bar, staring aimlessly into space.

She reported the presence to Colin, who was in the kitchen, and when he and the barmaid looked out to the bar, the old man with what the barmaid had described as "a leathery face," was gone.

Colin's brother, Malcolm, who was a partner in the business when they remodeled the old hotel in 1977, was a non-believer in all of this at first. He was there when the lights dimmed, the crane shook, the plug unplugged, etc., but remained the more stoic of the two.

That is, Colin said, until one day Malcolm made a startling admission.

"One day," Colin recalled, "Malcolm looked at me and said that there is something in this building. He told me that something had opened a door in front of him and stood in the doorway.

"He said he couldn't actually see whatever was

there, but he knew it was there. Admitting such a thing was not easy for him, so I had to believe him."

One of the most intriguing and incredible things to happen over the years was the episode of a stubborn barstool that would not budge when a barmaid nonchalantly attempted to slide it away while she was sweeping the floor.

The stool did not move, as if it was occupied by a weighty, unseen form.

Colin said the same thing has happened to him. He's tried to move a barstool, and on another occasion a chair, but neither would give an inch.

Frustrated, he gave up, took a few steps back in total bewilderment, and within a few seconds tried again, only to have the seats glide easily across the floor.

In the mid-1980s, the inn was purchased by Eric Wade.

What he bought was the restaurant business, the fine, old building, and, the ghosts.

Wade did his own amount of remodeling when he took the place over.

As he did so, he took Polaroid pictures of the progress. Lo and behold, a picture of the fireplace at which the Indian is said to have been killed revealed a strange glow. All present were certain there was no light in, or reflected into, the fireplace.

Wade also reported the footsteps, the levitating, the cantankerous doors, the cold spots and the light dimmings.

Most mysterious of all is a ghostly, white dove which has been seen by at least one patron, fluttering from thin air and back, in the dining room.

Robert Ripley made the phrase, "believe it or not," quite famous. You can believe what you have just read, or dismiss the various incidents as natural, not supernatural, occurrences.

But, if you're enjoying a quiet meal at the Inn at Maple Grove one evening and the chandelier starts to sway, the iron fireplace crane starts to shimmy, or the lucid image of a white dove takes wing as from out of nowhere, you'll believe...you'll believe!

•

A FINAL WORD

Even as you read this, the authors continue to fan out across the greater Lehigh Valley, where more tales of the supernatural lurk in the deep valleys, high hills, quiet villages and busy cities.

As has been the experience following the publication of seven previous volumes of ghost stories, even more dramatic and chilling accounts surface only after those who have lived through brushes with the supernatural realize someone out there will lend a sympathetic ear.

In the wake of the publication of this book, stacks of notes, tapes, and contact numbers remain in various stages of response and research. It is fully intended that a second volume of Lehigh Valley Ghost Stories will be published.

Anyone with a personal experience or knowledge of a haunting in the valley is invited to write to the publisher of this book and provide their name, address and contact telephone number. All such responses will be held in strictest confidence.

The authors and publishers of Ghost Stories of the Lehigh Valley hope you have enjoyed this book.

••

ABOUT THE AUTHORS

This is the tenth book written by Charles J. Adams III and David J. Seibold.

Adams, who also wrote three books on ghost stories in his native Berks County, Pa., is past president of the Reading Public Library and sits on the executive council and editorial board of the Historical Society of Berks County. Listed in "Who's Who in American Entertainment," Adams is morning radio personality at station WEEU in Reading, and is the chief travel correspondent for the Reading Eagle newspaper.

Seibold, a graduate of Penn State University, is an avid scuba diver and fisherman. He splits his time between homes in Reading, Pa., and Barnegat Light, N.J. He is a former commodore of the Rajah Temple Yacht Club and is a decorated Vietnam Campaign veteran. He is senior account executive at radio station WEEU and is active in many civic and social organizations.

As this book was being published, Adams and Seibold were researching and writing a book on ghost stories in Lancaster and surrounding counties, and plan a second volume of ghost stories of the Lehigh Valley.

• • •

Lehigh Valley Ghost Stories

ACKNOWLEDGEMENTS

Authors rarely succeed in thanking and recognizing all who have contributed in any way to the researching, writing and publication of a book.

The authors of this volume regret any omissions in this list, and extend sincere gratitude for all who have given of their time and knowledge for the compilation of Ghost Stories of the Lehigh Valley.

LIBRARIES: Allentown Public Library, Bethlehem Public Library, Memorial Library of Nazareth and Vicinity, Kutztown University Library, Reading Public Library, Kutztown Public Library, Library of Congress. BOOKS, MAGAZINES, NEWSPAPERS, ETC.: Allentown Call, Bethlehem Globe-Times, Easton Express, Reading Eagle, Lehigh Valley Life, Pennsylvania Magazine, The Pennsylvania German, the quarterly of the Pennsylvania German Society, History of Lehigh County, by Charles R. Roberts (1947); The Hex Woman, by Raube Walters; Lehigh Valley the Unsuspected, the newspaper writings of Dr. Richmond E. Myers as published by the Bethlehem Globe-Times and the Allentown Sunday Call-Chronicle from 1955-1972. ORGANIZATIONS: Northampton County Historical and Genealogical Society, the Pennsylvania German Society, Lehigh County Historical Society, Historic Bethlehem, Inc., Historical Society of Berks County, Historical Society of Pennsylvania.

●●●●

GHOST STORIES

OF THE

LEHIGH VALLEY

PHOTO GALLERY

Lehigh Valley Ghost Stories

High on a hill near Palmerton, this highly visible house is probably the best-known "haunted house" in the Lehigh Valley. Yet, despite its eeriness, there are no known ghostly tales associated with it. Looks, as they say, can be deceiving.

For many years, the "Lady in White" has made her ghostly presence known on the placid water of the Lehigh Canal in Walnutport. It is said her pallid form can be seen walking past this restored lock tender's house.

Lehigh Valley Ghost Stories

The historic State Theatre, on Northampton Street in Easton, is said to be haunted by at least one ghost, which has been nicknamed "Fred" by those who work or play in the theatre and must put up with the phantom's antics.

Lehigh Valley Ghost Stories

"...I've often heard it told, you can still hear Magnolia weeping along the Vineyard Road." The words are from an old sonnet which details the life, death and ghostly re-appearances of Magnolia Evans, for whom Magnolia's Vineyard restaurant in Guthsville was named.

Lehigh Valley Ghost Stories

Co-author David J. Seibold examines the grave of Elizabeth Bell Morgan on the grounds of the Easton Public Library. Strange events in the library have often been blamed on the ghost of the woman who was also known as "Mammy." The library was constructed on or near an ancient burial ground.

Lehigh Valley Ghost Stories

Getter's Island is visible between channels of the Delaware River near its confluence with Bushkill Creek in Easton. On that island, convicted murderer Charles Getter was executed, and on that island, it is said Getter's ghost still wanders.

Lehigh Valley Ghost Stories

The King George Inn, a popular dining spot along Hamilton Blvd. in Dorneyville, is said to be haunted by the ghost of an infant. Several employees have heard the eerie sound of a baby crying, and psychics have proclaimed the presence of ghostly energy.

The Brethren's House on the south campus of Moravian College in Bethlehem is one of several college buildings in which students and faculty members have reported hearing and seeing unexplained things.

Lehigh Valley Ghost Stories

The spirit of a young man who is thought to have died inside Comenius Hall at Moravian College in Bethlehem still creates a sensation. The building is one of several in Lehigh Valley-area colleges and universities which are said to be haunted.

The ghost of "Charlie" has teased patrons and employees of the Inn at Maple Grove, near Alburtis. The pesky wraith has made objects move, and created many harmless but frightening scenes in the restaurant. The inn has memorialized the ghost on its logo, menu and sign.

Lehigh Valley Ghost Stories

Barely discernible amid the tangle of trees and underbrush in a Williams Township woods is what legend has it is "Hexenkopf Rock." On this site, it is said, witches would cast spells, hexes and curses.

Lehigh Valley Ghost Stories

An indication of the strong beliefs in folklore which involves witchcraft, "powwowing" and "hexerie" is in the name of a road in Williams Township, south of Easton. Hexenkopf Road traverses what is called Hexenkopf, or "Witches Head."

Lehigh Valley Ghost Stories

Shadows, glows, disembodied sounds and strange events mark the presence of "Marvin," the resident spook at the Widow Brown's restaurant in Stockertown. Its sister restaurant, Widow Brown's in Wescosville, also harbors a ghostly resident.

Lehigh Valley Ghost Stories

With a little imagination, and a little knowledge about the tragic events which took place inside the Rusty Nail Tavern near Palmerton, it is easy to make out the ghostly, almost demonic, and indelible face in the door of a barroom cabinet.

Lehigh Valley Ghost Stories

Visible behind the Tiffany lamp and dining table at the Widow Brown's restaurant in Stockertown is a sealed doorway. Behind that door, legend has it a man hanged himself, setting off ghostly occurrences in the building.